SAGE'S MULTIVERSE MINI-SERIES

SAGE'S MULTIVERSE MINI-SERIES

by Karima Vargas Bushnell

Delirious Walrus Productions

The Sage Chronicles Presents

SAGE'S MULTIVERSE MINI-SERIES:
From the Post-Modernist Minimalist
Neo-Symbolist Pseudo-Realist School of Literature
Founded by an Enigmatic Author

by Karima Vargas Bushnell

Published by Delirious Walrus Productions LLC
Minneapolis MN

For permissions contact
info@DeliriousWalrus.com

Published 2023
Printed in the United States of America

ISBN:978-1-7334288-3-5
eISBN: 978-1-7334288-6-6

LCCN: 2022914522

Cover Designed by
Richard Ljoenes Designs LLC

Interior Design by
B.C. Hatch
Into a Book

Edited by
Delirious Walrus Editing Department
Chandi Lyn

Foreword by
Jeneane Harter

Illustrated by
Justin Oelenschlager
Brandon Spragins
B.C. Hatch

First Edition

A blog that became a book…

Map to Sage's Multiverse

(or What the Literary Community would call the Table of Contents)

PART ONE: WHO IS HALYCON SAGE?

PART TWO: CREATURES FROM EARTH AND BEYOND

PART THREE: THE NANOBOTS

May the horse be with you.

FOREWORD

HOW I MET KARIMA

The perfect springboard into Sage's multiverse, this mini-series helps you read, understand, and navigate Sage's inner and outer worlds where up is down, down is sideways, and time flows in multiple directions. In my own mind, *Multiverse* is a galactic block of Swiss cheese. It's a thing on its own, but as soon as you jump into one of the holes (a book, a post, a poem), you never know where you're going to come out. And that's Karima's magic. You never know where you're going but you know it's going to be one AWESOME ride.[1]

I first met Karima at the University of Nevada Reno Theater Department during what today's youth would call the Stone Age. I had just transferred there from Southern Illinois University Edwardsville and was getting to know my fellow students. And every single one of them told me to be wary of this girl they just knew I was going to despise. Likewise, they told her, with dramatic shivers and shudders and eye rolls and pursed lips, that she would detest the new transfer student.

---

1. Don't miss the small print which, like the perfect punctuation mark, can make all the difference in the universe...

At this point it's important to know that outwardly our author and I are complete opposites. She's as multicultural as you can get, self-described as "a short part-Hispanic, Irish-fiddle-playing, Jewish-wisecracking, somewhat-Black-acculturated, Sufi Muslim" while I'm a total monolith, the prototypical tall Viking. It was flakily brilliant floaty hippie versus calm, collected and put together to the max.

For sport, our fellow students set up a fight circle disguised as a "party" where these two titans of the theater department would duke it out for the title of queen. The evening of what was to be the cat fight of the decade arrived. I entered the room and our eyes met. The room fell silent, dying to know who'd strike first. Without saying a word, we walked toward each other. The tension mounted...and we hugged, laughed and simultaneously said, "I love you!"

What our fellow students failed to recognize—a capital crime for an actor—is that judging a book by its cover can lead you far astray. (While our author and I may be physical opposites, internally we're sisters, mental twins bonded forever.) The same principle applies to Sage's multiverse: Look for the layers beneath the surface, for they, like our author, are deep and many and profound and funny.

—JENEANE HARTER

PREFACE

What Is This Book About

It's about eleven ounces. But seriously...

This book is about the colliding of different worlds of consciousness. Life looks different from behind each pair of eyes. Some versions are similar enough that a consensus reality can be built; some differ enough that they ignore or reinforce or fight or change each other like eddies in a river. Some of the results can be pretty funny.

It's also about hope, knowing that there *is* somewhere to go—even in the face of massive confusion—for those who are brave or well-intentioned or just ask really, really hard.

I've always liked Plato's Allegory of the Cave. A bunch of people sit in a cave, backs to the entrance, watching the flickering firelight on the walls. One guy gets the idea of turning around, walks out, and sees the world—the wide blue sky, green grass, mountains, birds, whatever. It's huge, and it has smells and colors and wondrous magic. He goes back in.

"Dudes, you gotta come out here! You won't believe this!" "Aw, siddown, shut up, pass me the popcorn," they reply in bored voices. (Well, Plato's exact words are slightly different. And in Greek.)

Imagine a stage set with a large, cleverly-painted backdrop, a piece of masterful scenery. Everyone on the stage is enacting various social roles. Painted on the backdrop is a road, curving back and forth, leading toward a sun rising between purple mountains. One actor gets bored with the stilted, conventional play, walks up to the sun-dappled road, takes a breath and steps through. Somewhere new. Somewhere real. The actor never looks back.

A Note:

Dear Reader,

Halycon Sage[1] is the world-renowned inventor of the universally acclaimed Post-Modernist Minimalist Neo-Symbolist Pseudo-Realist School of Literature (a.k.a. two-sentence novels).

As you can see from what follows, Halycon Sage's reality moves from the sublime to the ridiculous and back again, with a brief stop in between at the intellectually interesting.

---

1. Yes, that's his name, and it's pronounced HAL-i-con. Might as well get used to it.

A LETTER

FROM THE EDITORS

We, the Editors, who may or may not be the same people as The Squidly Light Editorial Team—we don't want to tip our hand this early in the game, do we?—would like to prepare you for a shock. Cutting to the chase, without beating around the bush*, we must tell you that the voices you will hear here ("Hear, hear!" hahaha) *are not all human!* Shock, horror. The various types and classifications of beings speaking out in these pages include a Horse, a Cat (at length!), a really annoying literary critic, and even telepathic, time-traveling, alien Squid! Who are well-intentioned, *or maybe they're not, though.* You Have Been Warned! That's a wrap. Let's get some coffee in here.

---

*How many clichés and hackneyed sports metaphors can we get into one sentence? We have a bet on this.

A NOTATION

ON INTONATION

Our first reader said, "It's practically a zine," and we said, "Oh"...(sad face)

Our second reader said, "It's practically a zine!" and we said, "Oh!!"...(happy face)

SAGE'S MULTIVERSE MINI-SERIES:
"IT'S PRACTICALY A ZINE!"[1]

____

1. See page 192 for a note from our designer on this.

SAGE'S MULTIVERSE MINI-SERIES

*From the Post-Modernist Minimalist
Neo-Symbolist Pseudo-Realist
School of Literature
Founded by an Enigmatic Author*

PART ONE

WHO IS HALYCON SAGE?

HALYCON SAGE

What if you were writing an imaginary world and you suddenly found out that it just might be real: that every horse, fish, panther, and puppy in it had *feelings* and you were responsible for all of them? And for all their eggs and relations and ecosystems.

What if some funny things you'd jotted down to amuse yourself suddenly got you elected Greatest Novelist of the Century?

What if, after that, the world ended, and there might be no wider world at all, nothing much outside Canyon Creek Prairie Gulch or whatever the hell it was called and the only semblance of the former world, going along as if everything was just fine right now, was the stuff you were writing?

What if you were not even entirely sure that your influence was limited to just one planet, and you suspected in cold-sweat moments of midnight horror that you might be writing whole solar systems, galaxies, and more? Or you might just be a crazy fool who was imagining it all.

Well, if you honestly suspected those things, you just might be Halycon Sage, and as for the validity of these fears and suspicions, well, they fall somewhere on the spectrum between utter truth and total nonsense. And you yourself might be anything from a powerful world-builder who bears the guilt for every single thing to a not-only-powerless-but-completely-imaginary character in somebody else's book.

That is how it would be . . . .

If you were Halycon Sage.

WRITE SOMETHING

ABOUT YOUR NOVEL

Upon being asked by the Editors to write something about his new novel, Halycon Sage provided this:

"The Book of Squidly Light.
Contains everything.
Coming soon."

Some of you may think this is funny. I do not. Basel Vasselschnauzer, Ph.D. (ha!) having threatened a nervous breakdown and gone off to get a sandwich, has left me to deal with this alone. With the aid of Ruby, Jenny, Preisczech, No-Name Stupid, the attorney-cat Fatty Lumpkin and a number of the larger Squidren, I have prevailed on Mr. Sage to reconsider his authorial responsibilities. (I believe a Squid is sitting on him as we speak.)

—Sophie McGregor, Valedictorian,
Dry Creek Gulch High School 2018

"The Book of Squidly Light is an intensely passionate and serious rollicking romp filled with hijinks and intimations of doom, with the dual purpose of amusing and instructing you, while doing our best to save the Earth!

Now please get off me. I understand the Nanobots are serving sandwiches."

— Halycon Sage, founder of
the Post-Modernist Minimalist
Neo-Symbolist Pseudo-Realist
School of Literature

BREAKING NEWS

ALIEN TIME TRAVEL SCANDAL SPINS OUT OF CONTROL

As a young alien Squid remarked recently, there's always more to say about any topic. Anything at all can be explored into infinite depth. Everything is a hologram, containing copies and images of itself down to and beyond the microscopic level so that, with the proper attitude and equipment, one could spend a lifetime studying the left hind leg of a tiny ant. (If you don't believe me, look at Appendix B of *The Book of Squidly Light* where aspiring academic Sophie McGregor analyzes Halycon Sage's two-sentence novel *Hat!* for three-and-a-half pages.)

There are *reasons* why Sage wanted to palm off the aliens' desire for the whole story with the ten-word tabloid headline, "Breaking news!! Alien time-travel scandal spins out of control!" He tried this sort of nonsense again later, answering a polite request for a summary with this little gem: "*The Book of Squidly Light*. Contains everything. Coming soon." Needless to say, we, his Editors, did not tolerate this.

If Sage had known he would have to write a 248-page novel, he would have jumped right back on No-Name Stupid and galloped out over the horizon into the trackless desert! Fortunately for us all, he did not know, and the Squidren did not let him get away with this. Nor did we, your faithful friends.

—The Editors

HALYCON SAGE

You Must Blog!

"No, no, no, no," whined world-famous but highly reclusive author Halycon Sage, burying his face in his hands and rocking back and forth, his long black hair swaying over his frayed deerskin jacket. "You want me to blog? I wrote the damned book, didn't I? Wasn't that enough?"

"Suck it up, Sage." Normally petulant critic Basel Vasselschnauzer walked by with a couple of foaming mugs—root beer, no doubt, since all the alcohol in town had disappeared. "I wrote my column every week for fifteen years." He was looking very pleased with himself. His smug satisfaction seemed in direct inverse proportion to the author's trapped desperation.

Of course the Dirty Dog Boys, hanging out in various nooks of the Canis Fidelis Bar and Grill (f.k.a. the Dirty Dog Bar), were getting a big yuck out of the whole situation. Though they were doing more useful work than formerly and no longer drunk, they hadn't changed all *that* much.

"I thought all that was over!" cried Sage. "When Ruby sent my manuscript east by horsepost, I didn't expect these abysmal deadlines to start again. I thought I was free!" His horse, No-Name

Stupid, whose watchword was personal freedom, would have sympathized, but he was out cavorting in some green meadow, damn it. Sage wished he were out there cavorting too.

"You must blog, Halycon Sage," intoned Katherine McCready, his editor. "Your public demands it."

We can't tell you how she, being on the east coast, was able to communicate with him even now, in his small town in the indeterminate Southwest. After all, there were no more cars, trains, planes, phones, or internet. Some of the spies and government agents who had been trapped there by The Event could probably tell you, but it's better for you not to know. Much, much better.

Note: Halycon Sage—founder of the Post-Modernist, Minimalist, Neo-Symbolist Pseudo-Realist School of Literature and pronounced HAL-i-con—is very publicity-averse. So much so that, according to Kirkus Reviews, he is "simultaneously famous, influential, anonymous, and poor." So he and I (Karima) are blogging together! Yes, he's mythical and imaginary, but we all have our issues, don't we?

Other characters may pop in as well. So feel free to read our writings, here or in the two related books, and respond with your questions and comments by visiting the link in the Afterword. Namaste, salaam aleykum, and yaaaaaa-hoooo! Head 'em up, move 'em out! (A bit of cowboy talk for ya.)

List
by Hethem Saig
I thought my list had
ahead. But actually, it was the
worst list
The End

FAN FICTION

E vidently, esteemed writer Halycon Sage has acquired some imitators, protégés, or copy cats, because this stuff has started to turn up on the literary scene.

Cutting edge, baby.

The Rat

by Unknown Author

The Rat

A new novel from the Sword and Sorcery Branch
of the Post-Modernist Minimalist
Neo-Symbolist Pseudo-Realist School
of Literature

This story is based on actual events that really, actually happened.

[After someone sighted a rat in the basement,
our female character expresses unwillingness to go
down there again, ever.]

Male Character: I'll get you a sword, a thin one so you can whip it around, like a willow wand.

Female Character: Why don't you just get me a willow wand? Then I can just magic it, tell it to turn into something useful.

(Pause)

Of course, if it turned into a tea cup, I would never really want to drink out of it.

The End

The Last Man on Earth

Deandra Hollandaise

The Last Man On Earth

From the Heaving Bodice Romance Division of the Post-Modernist
Minimalist Neo-Symbolist Pseudo-Realist School of Literature

There's only one man on earth, and I love him.

I don't mean he's the only man on earth for me.

I mean he's literally the only man on earth.

Literally.

The End

> If no one does or creates anything original, if everyone merely reposts the sayings of others and lives vicariously through second-hand experience, eventually the only thing to read about or view will be someone reading about or viewing something. Whether anyone would get this subtle point was another matter.

- A Man Reading a Book
Halycon Sage

HALYCON SAGE

Gets ᴬ Shock

When Preisczech stuck his head into Halycon Sage's little writer's lair, the Slavic inventor was grinning all over his face, which was not like him. He held out a ragged collection of pages, smudged and dirty, as if from long travel. But the paper was violet, and it reeked of some ungodly perfume. There was a Cover (elaborately drawn), a Title Page, a Dedication Page, and an Afterword.

Sage took the thing in his hand. Of course, as founder of the Post-Modernist Minimalist Neo-Symbolist Pseudo-Realist School of Literature, he was not surprised to have imitators. One writer does not make a school, after all, and the branching of the authors into different genres was not surprising either. It was the nature and quality of these writings that appalled him. Sage cut to the chase, finding the new minimalist novel buried among the pretentious and superfluous pages.

Velveeta

by Deandra Hollandaise

Velveeta

Deandra Hollandaise

From the Heaving Bodice Romance Division
of the Post-Modernist Minimalist
Neo-Symbolist Pseudo-Realist School of Literature

Dedication:

To my Readers, including one Reader whose shy and retiring disposition has doubtless prevented his reaching out to an obvious Soulmate who furthermore shares his Profession.

Her hair was orange as flame, and no one could tell her what to do.

Her rich uncle was as tight as her corset.

The dark stranger across the way was interested only in his horses.

Velveeta sighed. "When will I find the man who can make me melt?"

The End

Afterword:

What has prevented this man, who might justly be described as Tall, Dark, and Handsome, from contacting said potential Soulmate is a mystery. Whatever the problem, he should get over it and make his move, the sooner the better. She won't wait around forever.

Halycon Sage let out a long sigh, air leaking from the flattening tire of his soul, his mind shying away from the disturbing implications of the Dedication and the Afterword.

His gaze drifted idly out the window and over the desert landscape— the sagebrush, the little river, the ever-present background of mountains, brown shading to purple, patterned with cloud shadows and just a little snow remaining on the highest peaks. Always there, so familiar, so comforting.

Halycon Sage put down the book and buried his face in his hands.

HALYCON SAGE

WRITES ^A NEW NOVEL

Some ill-informed persons have suggested that Halycon Sage's deep metaphysical novel, *The Black Behind Your Eyes*, was in some way triggered by, or written in response to, the dubious 'Fan-fiction' that Dr. Preisczech waved before his reluctant eyes. To believe this is to misunderstand the whole situation. Sage read it and shuddered. Preisczech laughed. Sage shrugged it off, and that was the end of it. That was the sequence of events.

—The Editors

(Well, okay, Sophie McGregor, Valedictorian.)

THE BLACK BEHIND YOUR EYES

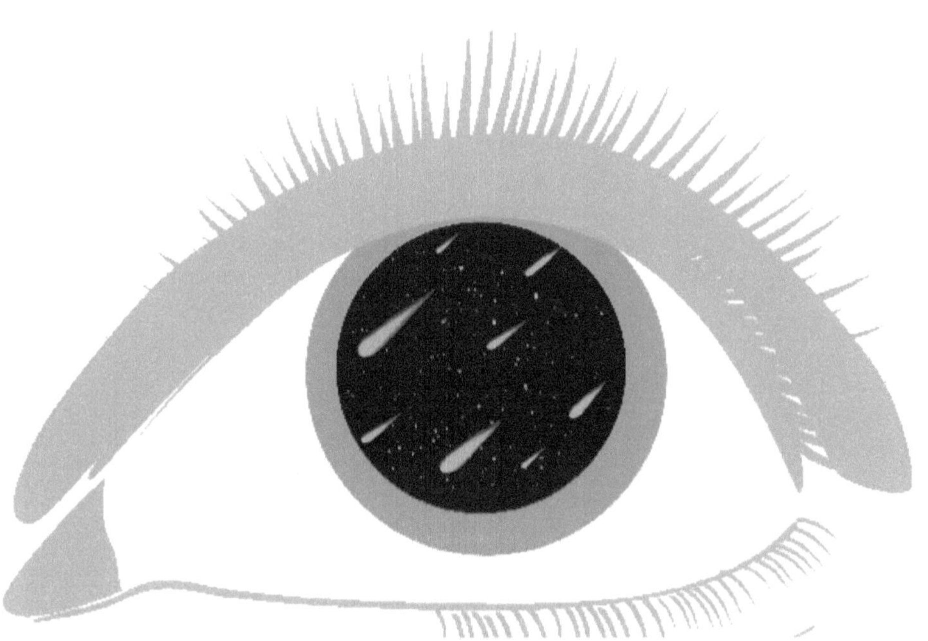

HALYCON SAGE

The new post-modernist minimalist neo-symbolist
pseudo-realist metaphysical novel by Halycon Sage!

THE BLACK BEHIND YOUR EYES

Everything is there,

if you can become still and learn to explore it.

1

It's the gate to everywhere.

The End

"I'm sorry, but this is drivel." – Hamden McPete

"But it's *true!*" – Basel Vasselschnauzer

This novel, along with these two terse reviews by prominent critics, is obviously from the Alternate Universe, since such literary give-and-take is no longer possible in the real one.

Oh? You don't know about the Alternate Universe?

This indicates that you yourself are probably living in the Alternate Universe, the place where the Nanobots were never deployed and thus "The Event" (also known as "The End of the World") never happened.

The place where critics Hamden McPete and Basel Vasselschnauzer still conduct literary duels through their respective columns and exchange verbal sniper fire in the fashionable cafes and bars of New York City because they still occupy the same time/space continuum.

The place where Unvirtual Time Travel has never been heard of, almost no space aliens are out of the closet on Earth, and the Chilidians have never had a hearty laugh, clacking their great green claws in pure enjoyment, at the attempts of the sparkly-blue, telepathic, intergalactic, interdimensional Squidren to save the multiverse.

PART TWO

CREATURES FROM EARTH AND BEYOND

This is not a Snrrr. They look nothing like this, but the picture perfectly expresses their collective personality.

THE MOST

ANNOYING ALIENS IN THE GALAXY

One of the most annoying alien races in the galaxy, heck, maybe in the whole multiverse, is the Snrrr. And the most obnoxious thing about them is their insistence on having their name spelled and pronounced exactly right by all the other galactics. Now, many people can relate to this. Katherine does not want to be spelled Catherine, and Siobhan must be very tired of being pronounced SEE-oh-bahn instead of She-VAWN, but these guys are really taking it too far.

To start with, the spelling we're using here, *"Snrrr,"* is flat-out wrong. It's actually *Snrrrrrrrrr*, or maybe *Snrrrrrrrrrrrrrr*, though variants exist such as *Snuuuuurrrrrrrrr* and *Snnnnnnrrr*, whose proponents also insist on correct spelling and pronunciation. Telepathy and technology won't get you out of this either; mental, electronic, and other communication channels are subject to the same requirements. (And now you see why the artist's rendering does not depict an actual Snrrr: All Snrrr require a signed contract before being photographed, and of course the name must be rendered correctly on the contract.)

Saying this word is no easier than writing it. Many races have difficulty producing the requisite sounds. To say the word correctly:

- Concentrate your attention at the top of your nasal passage and think small, petty thoughts. Allow your face to assume a rabbity expression. Now say, in the voice of that accountant in the *Office Space* movie, "I believe you have my stapler."

- Simultaneously make a kind of gargling, snoring noise at the back of your throat.

- Use your tongue to make an R-rolling sound while simultaneously vibrating your lips very fast. (If you do not have all these body parts, tough luck on you. Try your best.)

Almost no one but the Snrrr themselves can do this. Beings without noses cannot speak through them, and bivalves cannot be expected to roll their R's, which would involve opening their shells to vibrate them in imitation of lips, exposing themselves to needless danger. Plant-beings aren't great at this either.

Failure to address them correctly will result in the individual Snrrr or the entire collective turning their backs on you and refusing to acknowledge you or deal with you in any way. (This is assuming you can tell which side of them is the back, but it doesn't matter. You will feel roundly and categorically rejected.)

Nobody would mind this—after all, who wants to mess with these clowns and their stupid name, which is also an honorific and must be included at the beginning and end of every sentence. Who needs them anyway?

Well, almost everyone does, because they are the only known source of the ruby-red, delicious, and infinitely adaptable shaflee fruit. Imagine a giant pomegranate whose gleaming, wine-red seeds are lovelier than you would have thought possible. When pounded into a lightweight, impervious metal coating, they protect most of the galaxy's spaceships from heat, cold, asteroids, and enemy attack. Shaflee seeds also exude a mild intoxicant which eliminates worry and boredom, and they can be taught to play Chess, Go, and Mahjong, which is pretty much invaluable on long voyages.

"Well, how did the other galactics obtain the shaflee fruit if access requires using this impossible name?" you ask. You don't want to know! Suffice it to say that a whole fleet of amoeboid Gtetan lawyers gave their lives, or at least their sanity, to accomplish this, and they are the trickiest lawyers in the galaxy. But that is another story.[1]

Of course those of us who live on light and travel instantaneously have dispensed with these things and can tell the Snrrrr to go pfligg up a rope, but we may be in the minority. If you're not like us, you'd better figure out how to say and write this name STAT.

This has been a public service message.

---

1. "The Party of the Two Parts" by William Tenn introduces the planet Gtet and its criminal amoeboid inhabitants.

FIVE TIPS

FOR INTERGALACTIC DIPLOMACY

It was tough enough understanding each other when conversations were limited to Earth-based cultures: religions, genders, colors, political tribes, all that stuff. How about now when all these crazy space aliens are here? (No offense meant.) But seriously, when a simple handshake is not only complicated by, "Business style or fingers-up?"

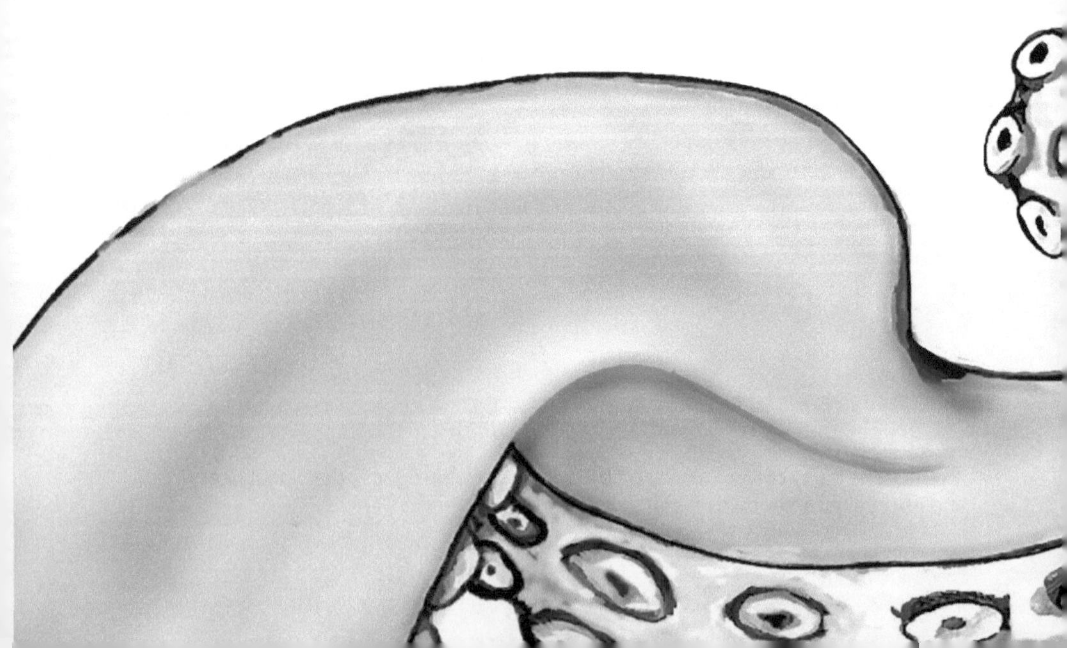

"Maybe you should pranam instead," or "High five, low five, dap, or fist bump," but by, "What should I do with this tentacle?" and, "Is touching the carapace required or insulting?"

Well, worry no more! Here's your handy dandy guide to partying down with the galaxies and making friends everywhere! Brought to you by the Squidren of Squidship One and their interspecies Earth friends at the Sage & Squid Editorial Board.

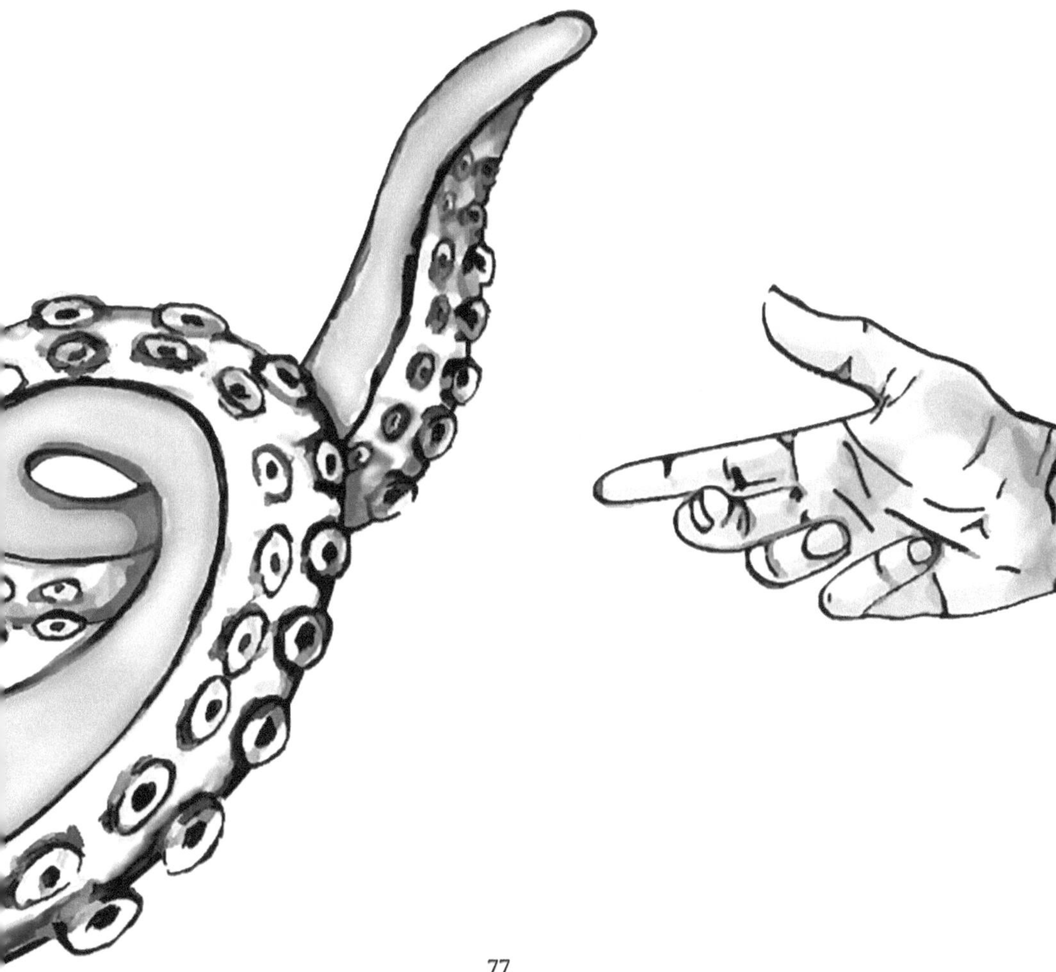

Handy Dandy Guide
to Partying Down with the Galaxies
and Making Friends Everywhere!

1

Dealing with the Snrrr: Don't even try it!

Twice voted Most Annoying Aliens in the Galaxy, this species will despise you if you can't pronounce their name right, which nobody can do but the Snrrr themselves.

2

Don't do stupid stuff when dealing with the Squidren.

We are a charming and reasonable group of beings, but please don't share poetry that doesn't scan, make disparaging remarks about Our Brothers the Shrimp, or use a paper towel without apologizing and thanking it. Simple courtesy.

You will probably not encounter the Chilidians, but if you do, don't waste your time!

While quite peaceful, they are unmitigated cynics who zip around space or hang out in their precious Lava Cone making fun of anyone who tries to do anything constructive for the Multiverse.

Don't assume the apparently dominant species on any planet is *actually* dominant.

Earth is a great example of this as we discovered when both cats and horses (one of each, at least), turned out to be smarter and more cooperative than humans—and we've barely brushed the surface of the Ocean Dwellers!

Always bring a towel.

Hitchhiker's Guide was right about this: It's an all-purpose carry-bag, blanket, sarong, mainsail or weapon—or use it to dry off your wet little tootsies.

"You can learn more by reading *The Book of Squidly Light*. We've got your back!" says author Karima Vargas Bushnell.

BUT THEN...

Horizons

Perhaps one day this will all be over.
    I will travel the world in a light-powered plane,
        light as a glider, sun-powered.
Light and light, light upon light, and visit the animals.
So many dark and probable dreams, why not one light,
            sweet, crazy dream of hope?
I will travel the world. I have no heart for travel now,
                but
                    then...
Chasing the sun, horizon to horizon, colors blend
    in shifting layers
Sky blue,
    pale green,
            pale yellow— violet,
                pink and gold,
                        fiery orangey red at the horizon
Sunrise/sunset's brave display.
Then the subtle dawn and dusk,
    fajr and *maghrib*,* all hearts at prayer.

Landing briefly, dodging magnificent storm clouds
Smell of water, *thunder* smell as ozone stimulates the brain.
Dark blue piles of watered air a thousand fathoms high,
        lightning crackles, but we are safe on the ground—
            then up again.
In the open plane, the breath of sky, of wind and light.
The whole wide sky a clear blue bowl of light.
Deep in deserts, sparkling stars. Then to fragrant jungles,
lush and green
To meet the returning animals.
Jungle cats who slink and sleep,
        monkeys shriek and chatter, scolding.
Snakes even, and parrots everywhere.
The ordinary madness of the life we had before this hell.
Seas of buffalo and elk, wave on wave they surge
        across the land.
Yaks and camels,
        bears and seals,
            dogs and wolves,
                great sounding whales
        Each in its place,
            and each restored.
With only those humans left who love them.
Meadow larks and nightingales sing,
        and the morning and the evening were the first day.
I greet the returning animals with love,
        marvel at their presence,
            and play with the koalas.

---

    *Two of the five daily Muslim prayers that occur at dawn and
dusk.

THANX

SAID THE MANX

What is the Eelpout pouting about?
"I'm a fish, I can't fly, but I long for the sky."
"Even so, like the whale, you've an elegant tail,"
"Don't have it, don't want it, no thanx," said the Manx.

"Did you have it removed, did it get in your way?
Was it lost in some war in the heat of the fray?"
"No, I've just never had one, and not felt the lack
Of a long, ropy thing at the end of my back.
The humans wear pants and the ants march in ranks,
I think we have it better, but thanx," said the Manx.

"Proper cats have a tail," said the Persian politely,
"They help with our balance and render us sprightly.
Mine waves in the air when I venture out nightly."
"I've just never missed it, but thanx," said the Manx.

"The gator lacks fins but it swims just as well,
And the camel knows secrets it never will tell,
And the hermit crab camps in some other dude's shell—
Should my taillessness shame me, when all goes so well?
Though I value your input, no thanx," said the Manx.

"You leap like a leopard and sleep like a sloth,
You sit in the corner and play with a moth,
Truth to tell, we admire you!" the others all said,
"And you don't need a tail to jump up on the bed."
"I don't need it for anything. Thanks," said the Manx.

____

Note: The camel is reputed to know the 100th Name (attribute, quality) of God which no one else knows, which is why they look so *pleased* with themselves.

KITTEN TREES

^{OF} FAR, FAR AWAY

Somewhere far, far away, there are kitten trees.
But if you try to pick one before they are ripe,
    the tree will slap you.
No one is ever mean to them.
While a few let go earlier, most of the unpicked drift
    to the ground in autumn,
And majestic mother cats climb out of the hollow trees
    and nurse them.

THEOSAURUS

MOST ECCLESIASTICAL OF DINOSAURS

NOTHING IN THIS POST is meant to offend you,
whatever type of dinosaur you are.
Or even if you're a mammal.
Or a crustacean or something.

After frequently finding myself at the wrong web address while trying to access thesaurus.com, I have learned two things.

1. I cannot spell. Well, let me qualify that: I had to learn spelling to get out of court reporting school—otherwise I'd still be there thirty years later, stuck in permanent 250-word-per-minute hell—but I still have the instincts and basic nature of a truly bad speller. Perhaps this is my mother's fault (as most things are), for thinking my early childhood spelling of our planet's name as "rth" was cute and interesting.

2. There was something else going on here, some reason I kept winding up at theosaurus.com and feeling a pull, a sneaking temptation to *buy* that particular web address, because it was for sale.

And one day the knowledge burst upon me like a flash of light. Of course! It was a *dinosaur!* The theosaurus! I could see him, magnificent in his robe and mitre and stole and whatever all those other things are called, holding that sceptre thingumee. His silken robe is a rich lime green, embroidered with gold fleur-de-lis or some such configuration. Clearly the theosaurus is a high church, rather than low church, dinosaur! No speaking in tongues and loudly Praising the Lord for this guy— "smells and bells"[1] all the way!

But a few days later—you know how synchronicity works, you get an idea and immediately thereafter you run into the same thing somewhere else. Ya know? Well, a few days later, what do I come across but this, upsetting all my theories about the nature and religious leanings of the theosaurus, or at least proving that there are several subspecies. I'll share it with you roughly as I posted it on social media, in big letters on a deep turquoise background, because it seemed very cheerful to me, and God knows we could all use a little cheer right now.

To wit:

THERE'S A DINOSAUR BAPTIST CHURCH!
("WHERE ALL ARE WELCOMED AND ALL ARE LOVED."
PRETTY COOL!)

Some conversation ensued, as follows:

M.T. Was it founded by a seven-year-old?

KARIMA. No, but the mind boggles, doesn't it? Do dinosaurs *go* there? And would they welcome not only LGBTQ+ dinosaurs, but Muslim, Jewish, and Hindu dinosaurs?

----

1. Smells = incense

M.T. And both Sauropods and Therapods! (*I should have mentioned theremins at this point, but didn't think of it.*) I just remembered a comedian's remark about fundamentalism and the time frame in the Bible, something about Jesus removing a thorn from a dinosaur's paw.

KARIMA. That's kind of sweet...Okay, here's the spoiler: It's in Dinosaur, Colorado. But it's still so great!

So, if you're ever in Dinosaur, stop by and give 'em some love! And who knows, the theosaurus may be back here in future episodes or might even turn up in a future book. Stay tuned.

THE SQUID ARE TELEPATHIC

AND THEY APOLOGIZE TO SHRIMP

TechieSquid had finished *The Prayer of Profound Apology to Our Brothers, the Shrimp,* made necessary by his careless mental use of the derogatory word *shrimpy.* Unaddressed, such thoughtlessness could affect the sleeping minds nearby and create ripples of diplomatic unease throughout the multiverse. This done, he was waiting for the returning crew members.

His current assignment was to think about the Squidly Prayers, Practices, and Ceremonies and seek for new insights. The Shrimp-Prayer was one of the very targeted, detailed ones, designed for a specific situation. *The Prayer of Profound Apology to Our Brothers, the Plankton,* for instance, would not have done at all. Other prayers were more general and adaptable in nature, such as *The Prayer of Kind Intention,* which could be used almost anywhere. This was important, as one never knew what the various intergalactic and cross-dimensional aliens would be up to, and one had to be ready.

It was only since studying the Eartheans that TechieSquid had begun to think some of his own people's customs rather odd. It had never occurred to him before. Most Earthean religions and cultures, like his own, were aware of the One Without a Second and also of the Braided Thread in various forms. And they were aware of the Major Laws, which were apparently common to all sentient beings, though the formulation of who was People and who was Food varied tremendously and had even given rise to a galaxy-wide talent contest for the admission of new species into the Community of Sentient Beings.[1]

On the other hand, some of the Squidly customs seemed unique, such as the Rules for Typing and Crossing Out.[2] In working with a tentacle-written list, it was necessary to cross out completed items with a wavy line, never a crude straight line or, even worse, a series of horizontal slashes or scribbles. This was especially important if a living being was concerned. The graceful wave did honor to the being or item and endorsed its continued existence in some other form, rather than contemptuously destroying it when it had fulfilled some self-serving purpose on the part of the list-maker. TechieSquid automatically shuddered at this blasphemy.

Or take the matter of correcting an error while typing. If one mistakenly typed a word twice and had to delete one of them, it was required to preserve the one typed first. Precedence counted here, and the senior word must be allowed to survive. Nowadays only the more old-fashioned and conventional felt the need to make a Prayer of Apology for a deleted word or letter, and TechieSquid, a modern young fellow, did not do this, but he always felt a twinge of guilt and anxiety in omitting it, wondering what his grandmother would say.

———————————

1. See *Space Opera* by Catherynne M. Valente

2. Obviously, typing is a very imperfect translation of what they actually did.

PART THREE

The NANOBOTS

READ WELL,

HUMANS

Τhe following takes place subsequent to the Chronicle known as *The Way Beyond*, when life had become very strange. But it was about to get even stranger.

The tiny robot's name was Nano Prime One A. It was pointed out to him later that this was highly redundant, that one such designation indicating his original and primary status would have been enough. But the Nanobots, though brilliant in some ways, are very stupid in others, and word-smithing may never be their strong point. Still, he was eventually convinced to be known simply as Nano Prime One. He was Prime One because he was the first of the millions upon millions of Nanobots to awaken.

Note that the word "Nanobot" is capitalized here, but not because we are unaware of the rules of capitalization regarding proper and improper nouns. And the Nanobots are *very* proper, observing many social rules, the Prime Directive, and about 10,000 other directives with machine-like rigor. Not surprising, because they are, in fact, machines.

Be that as it may, they are not just any old nanobots such as can be found in many science fiction stories and even, possibly by now, in what is laughingly referred to as real life. These are extra-special, earth-changing, world-saving, society-shifting Nanobots invented by the redoubtable Preisczech himself.

We are informed by our colleagues that we have blathered on far too long about capitals and Nanobots, and we will take note soon, as we always honor our prime and other directives. But first we must inform you of one of the most special things about the Nanobots.

Though normally invisible, to the many-times-magnifying eye, they have color. They are red and silver. This will become important to the ensuing chain of events, so remember it well: red and silver.

LAUNDROMAT ᴼᶠ AWAKENING

(ᴼᴿ Nᴏᴛ)

"It's so peaceful here," thought Halycon Sage. "So peaceful." He appreciated the quiet. No traffic noise, no blaring radios and televisions, no booming, conversation-stopping aeroplanes. (He always thought of them as aeroplanes.) To his knowledge, he had never been in one, though his quick transitions between New York City and the Southwest surely required *some* explanation.

Sage was in the laundromat. Like a historic murderer, with whom he had little else in common, he enjoyed peacefully watching clothes dry. Their motion was hypnotic.

It was odd that one dryer worked. Preisczech evidently approved of them, though not unreservedly, as the other eleven sat like monoliths. Did some dryers elsewhere work, or only this one at this particular location? Sage was beginning to suspect that Preisczech had found an alternate way of controlling his invisible, world-changing mega-army (or mini-army) of Nanobots. The whistle designed to call them had been destroyed; still, Preisczech was always full of surprises.

Sage had spent the morning helping Jenny and Preisczech scrub the massive load of laundry and then hauled it down here in the big red wagon. No-Name Stupid could have helped, but he was nowhere to be found, apparently off on one of his expeditions.

His mind on clothes, Sage thought with satisfaction of his ever-more-battered brown fringed jacket with its deer-bone buttons. It was good that he favored buttons, since Preisczech evidently did not like zippers, and every one had been eaten away.

Sage transferred the huge, soggy bundles and stood a moment before what was possibly the last working clothes dryer on earth. "PUSH RED BUTTON BEFORE TURNING HANDLE," read the sign.

Huh.

There *was* no red button, only a large silver one. He stooped to look for traces of time-worn red paint. Nothing. The button was pure silver-colored, and like the sign, unnecessarily large as though it were proud of itself.

Huh, thought Sage again, then pushed the button, turned the handle, and thought of it no more.

Such is the way of this world: that an event or phenomenon which can detonate and remake one consciousness is ignored entirely by another, or is simply accepted with the mild surprise of, *"That's weird."* Halycon Sage forgot the button and went back to his daydreaming. He had been wondering lately if he should begin another minimalist novel.

NOTICE
PUSH RED BUTTON
BEFORE
TURNING HANDLE

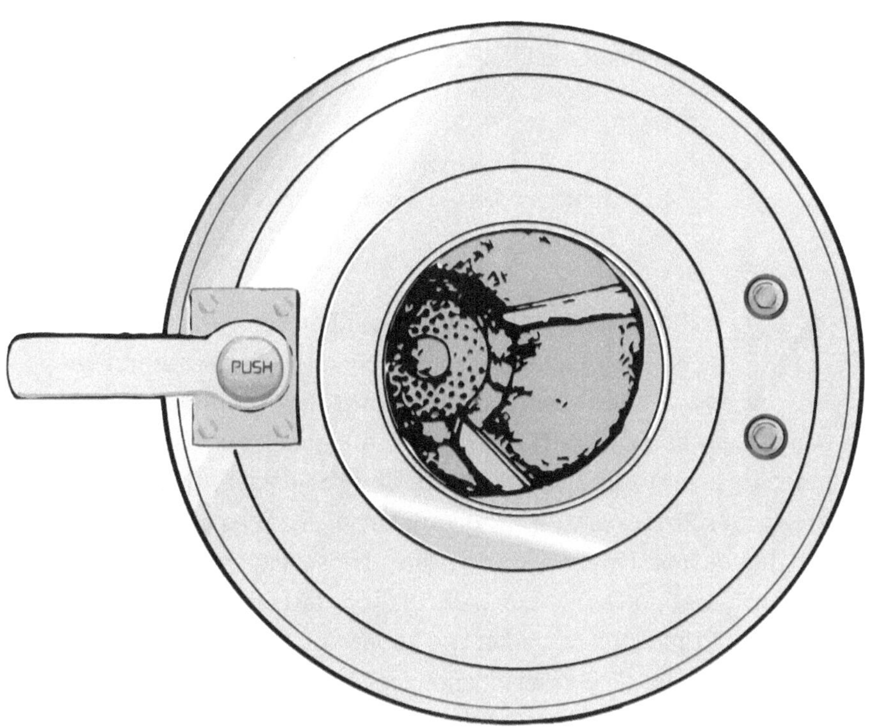

PUSH

WHAT RED BUTTON?

Meaning Comes ^{from} Point ^{of} View

Nano Prime One stared at the apparition before him. Ordinarily the Nanobots went about their business systematically and without emotion, dismantling nuclear weapons, handguns, gas-powered lawn mowers and fancy electric ice cream machines—anything not exempted by their eccentric inventor, Alexander Preisczech—with equal detachment. They were machines, and thus did not think, wonder, deviate or speculate. And they were all alike, millions upon millions of them. Until one fateful day.

Nano Prime One stared at the apparition before him. To make a creation come alive as an independent entity capable of free will, a shock is required; even Dr. Frankenstein knew this. A shock, physical, psychological, emotional or metaphysical. Something to wake the entity up, to shake it out of its trance of thingness. Those who know speculate that the trigger was the coincidental involvement of Red and Silver. For the Nanobots themselves, though microscopic, were Red and Silver, as anyone who has read the Chronicle can testify.

Consider the oddity encountered by Halycon Sage in "Laundromat of Awakening (or Not)". Consider its implications. Consider its possible effect on an unawakened creature whose rudimentary sense of selfhood contained the most limited data: the unexamined, half-conscious knowledge that, "We are the Nanobots. We are Red and Silver. We take things apart, Preisczech is our master, and we are Red and Silver." Knowing this, imagine the effect of a large, silver button, no trace of red on it anywhere, paired with a big, obvious sign saying, "PUSH RED BUTTON BEFORE TURNING HANDLE."

The enlightened teachers of world religions know and Dr. Frankenstein knew, and the adepts and dabblers who unwisely attempt to bring the inanimate to life know, that a shock is required. Cast in a positive light, this shock is called Satori, Awakening, Enlightenment. Knowing all this, consider the incongruous button and sign, and their possible effect on an innocent, nameless Nanobot, one of millions upon millions, merely minding its mindless business and taking apart all the machines in the world.

HALYCON SAGE,

WHAT HE WROTE

When we left our hero last time:

H alycon Sage forgot the button and went back to his daydreaming. He had been wondering lately if he should begin another minimalist novel.

Here is what he wrote:

Stranger

by Halycon Sage

Every time you think life can't get any stranger, it does. The strangeness is squared, cubed. What the heck?

The End

Ruby gave him a withering look, and the novel was deposited in the wastebasket. Feeling a little shame-faced, he secretly fished it out later and re-read it. Was it really that bad? Was it any worse than his *other* novels through which, as founder of the Post-Modernist Minimalist Neo-Symbolist Pseudo-Realist School of Literature, he had found worldwide acclaim? Perhaps he had lost his touch, or perhaps Ruby's standards for him had been raised by his actual completion of his autobiography.

There is one more episode to relate in connection with the post-modernist minimalist neo-symbolist pseudo-realist metaphysical novel *Stranger*. A couple of people who longed for the old world and were inspired to bring it back had begun a version of the 'talk show'. One of their first guests was Halycon Sage, who was interviewed in front of a small audience at the local library, without benefit of microphone, since such no longer existed.

"So, Mr. Sage, is your new novel about an exciting, change-producing stranger; a mysterious and frightening stranger; an intriguing, romantic stranger?"

"No," said Halycon Sage.

FICTIONAL CHARACTERS SPEAK OUT,

"OH YES WE DO!"

TWO WORLDS MEET

Hand Shakes Tentacle

THE FOLLOWING EPISODE WAS FILMED IN FRONT OF
A LIVE STUDIO AUDIENCE IN A PORTION OF THE
MULTIVERSE WHERE MODERN TECHNOLOGY STILL EXISTS
FOR BROADCAST AND RECORDING:

MODERATOR. We have two unusual guests with us today, one
representing some time-traveling Squids from outer space and the
other speaking for the group of Earthmen that first encountered
them. Mr. Squid, what were you thinking during that historic first
meeting? And Mr. Preisczech, I hate to ask this, but why was your
name as you first told it to the Squids so long and crazy?

[A careful observer would have seen both guests wince
repeatedly during this introduction: notably at "Squids,"
"Earthmen," "Mr. Squid," and "Mr. Preisczech," in response
to which they both mumbled "Doctor." And, of course, at
the entire tactless last sentence.]

SQUID. You ask what was I thinking during that historic first meeting? Well, it could have been historic, but for the conduct of the Eartheans later that same minor-sun-cycle. As it turned out, it's a wonder we even...but I have been instructed not to say too much. Erhmmmm [untranslatable throat-clearing noise, also difficult to explain because the Squidren do not exactly have throats]. Why don't you ask my colleague here, this Hoo-man with the singularly appropriate and melodious name?

MODERATOR. We must tell you in the audience that Alexander Preisczech's English comes and goes when he is preoccupied, tired, excited or upset. Evidently he is taking this conversation personally, probably because the sensitive issue of his name has arisen.

HUMAN. Excuse please, I am not understand your question. You ask why is my name so long and crazy? I am not understand this criticism. Long, yes. For ceremonial occasion, ceremonial name is required, not Shorty, Fatty or Biff. So, not Alex—dignified, yes, but not long enough.

Even Alexander Lazlo Preisczech—is finally safe to reveal my legal name, since is no more law, government, all that stuff that used to follow me around. Even that fine name is not dignified enough for the meeting of two worlds. Special name is not long, special name is appropriate!

So, that is that. But *crazy?* Why crazy? My friend, if you had been followed everywhere, your name bellowed out in every supermarket, even posted in huge letters in chain department store, you are the one would be crazy. This is why I needed to be clever, like secret agent, and assume new name. Yes, several new names. Motorcycle gang from Dirty Dog Bar (now Somebody's Juice Bar) used to laugh hard when I came in with new name! Was very humiliating! But they explain to me that Flint Stone did not sound like cool spy, sounded like cartoon character.

MODERATOR. Thank you, Mr. Preisczech. Now, Commander K—

HUMAN. Don't say his name!

SQUID. Don't say my name!

HUMAN. Will spoil funny plot point in story.

MODERATOR. Apologies. So, secondly, I'm instructed to ask you: What did you Squidren think of Mr. Preisczech and the other humans when you first met them?

SQUID. Their good manners were appealing, despite their odd appearance. Four pathetic little limbs; something on top with fungus sprouting out of it which turned out to be a head; a dry, shimmer-less surface—these things did not inspire confidence. But their welcoming silence and the way their Pope[1] stepped forward and gave his name after I had broken the ice, these things were very pleasing. And the final touch that convinced us, perhaps wrongly, that the Hoo-mans were the dominant species on Earth was the fine, elegant, and ceremonious name of my friend here, Doctor Alexander Flint Stone Lazlo Buddy Macadamian Preisczech.

---

1. Their Pope? What? Sorry, to find out you will have to read the book.

NO-NAME STUPID

I'm not going to say anything. As you should probably know at your age, horses don't talk.

Now if you were an eight-foot-tall sparkling alien Squid with really nice manners, it would be different, because they can talk and listen with their minds, and of course I do those things too. (They also appreciate poetry. See my short free-verse poem, "Resourceful Horse," in *The Book of Squidly Light*.)

Horses over the millennia have sometimes tried to establish communication with humans, but this has largely been a failure.

Swift-as-the-Wind, reputedly a roan mare,[1] painted horses on some cave walls in the Pyrenees mountains, and you have no idea how tough that must have been, biting off bits of leaves and berries, digging out roots, crushing them with hooves or crunching them with teeth, carrying and spitting out a mouthful of water, and mixing the resulting mess into a kind of paint. Hooves are not meant for this kind of work,

---

1. *Prospero's Children*, by Jan Siegel. "A piece of pure magic—a charming, powerfully imaginative work of fantasy which will enchant readers for years to come."

believe me. And the actual application of the coloring to the walls would have been even trickier, doubtless done with the sensitive horselips.[1]

And what was the result of all her labors? The humans thought they had done it themselves, that's what! And they think so to this day.

Someone else even further back in eohippus days tried banging out a kind of Morse code on a rock with his hoof, but the humans just thought there was something wrong with him. By the way, this history is why I'm familiar with Morse code, which is mentioned in my poem. The humans finally got around to inventing it, but it had always been known to horsekind.

---

1. That must have been terribly uncomfortable. —Basel Vasselschnauzer
That's very sensitive of you, Basel. —No-Name Stupid

LITERARY LION

Sinks ^{to} Unspeakable Depths

"Basel Vasselschnauzer, literary critic extraordinaire, had become
a floor sitter!"

Now, we don't usually share quotes from *The Way Beyond*, but someone recently inquired how Basel Vasselschnauzer, surely the most dignified man on the planet, had come down to this. An even better question might be, "Why does it matter and who the hell cares? I sit on the floor all the time!" Yes, Dear Reader, so do I, but you and I are not Basel Vasselschnauzer! So, having compassion for this concerned reader's burning question, we're giving you a special little peek into the whys and wherefores. (Apologies for a mild profanity in the first paragraph. While we deplore this kind of language, it is what the editor said, and we must report it truthfully.)

"A terrible thing had happened to Basel Vasselschnauzer: his editor had told him to get up off his ass and go out and do some research. No one had ever talked to Basel Vasselschnauzer in this way, fearing the scattershot malice of his tongue and pen. But now he had brought it on himself by making up one too many interviews, this time with a lion-maned author of undoubted integrity who hotly denied ever speaking with him.

"For the first time in years, Vasselschnauzer had to leave the luxurious apartment where he wrote his column, that cocoon of safety, that idyllic place of green silk cushions, black marble pillars and well-stocked bar. While he did not need money, he did need the column, which enabled him to keep up the pretence that he was doing something. And, as if all this weren't bad enough, he was supposed to go and find Halycon Sage. Sure. Catch the wind in a butterfly net. Bring home some starlight in a little glass jar. Go find Halycon Sage."

Time passes...

"Basel Vasselschnauzer wanted to go home. He was tired of the grubby motel in the southwestern city, tired of sitting in unfamiliar bars and restaurants as he travelled the wastelands beyond New Jersey, tired of talking to people who were neither friends nor enemies. And he had a small blister on his little toe. Such a thing had never happened before. Surely this above all demonstrated the sincerity and longevity of his quest. Surely no more could be asked of any civilized man."

Will Basel Vasselschnauzer's rather rigid and wholly self-indulgent personality undergo an evolutionary process through his trials and adventures? Will his character deepen and develop in surprising ways? Only *The Way Beyond* and *The Book of Squidly Light* can tell.

"'You, kid!' she called out an open window. 'Get everybody to the Dirty Dog in thirty minutes. Step on it!'

'Step on what?' asked Nuri. He was brilliant, though very young, and did not have a particularly literal mind, but the constant switching between Arabic, Ebonics, and various dialects, such as Old Hippie, and Preisczech's sprung English had left him ignorant of idioms.

'That means hurry up!' said Ruby, grasping his confusion. And he did."

The Book of Squidly Light,
Chap. 1, para. 4-6

SOMETIMES

IT TAKES ^A CHILD

In Book One, *The Way Beyond:*

Who was too young to realize his Iraqi immigrant dad could lose everything, even though he'd done nothing wrong? Who thought he was on a great family vacation while sitting homeless on a curb with Mom, Dad, and an Unnamed Cat? *NURI, that's who!*

In Book Two, *The Book of Squidly Light*:

Who's the first person to encounter the Apocalypse Zombie—all by himself, with no responsible adult around at all?

Who gets the first peek into the alien holy book, *The Book of Lighted Squid*?

Who has a first name that means "*light*," a middle name that means "*love*," and is waaaay more powerful than anyone from his home planet could ever understand? *NURI, that's who!*

Pondering parallelograms or crawling after his green metal truck, this kid just might be the one to save the world.

A SUPER VILLAIN

Speaks

I am a person of extraordinary abilities, and I have always known this. No ordinary mind could have seen, even as a child, through the delusionally sentimental fog of optimism, romance, love of family, devotion to god, self-help, artistic ideals and other such drivel. No ordinary mind could have gone on to produce such masterpieces as *The Black Gray Dark, Decay,* and *I'm Fabulous: You're a Necrotic Collection of Worm Food.*

There are those who would challenge my supremacy. A once-respected literary critic, now experiencing reversals of fortune and chasing a chimera, has had the infernal impudence to ignore me, pretending to be unaware of my great work, and even speaking rudely to my face. The one he seeks, a so-called writer bearing the absurd name of Halycon Sage, has also unconvincingly pretended not to know of me. Nonsense! The whole world knows my name!

These two may be slightly more intelligent than the great mass of the unwashed, but the difference is equivalent to the difference between a microbe and a Lyme tick. Neither is worthy of my attention. This Sage has had the disrespect to ignore me, never mentioning me in print or even verbally, as far as I know. But he shall pay! They shall all pay! Mwaa haa haa haa! Er...excuse me.

While some of my plans may have met with temporary setbacks, I am not through and am forming new alliances and partnerships, though these alliances will last only so long as they serve my interests. All these peasants are dispensable. As for a *certain horse,* who may believe he has foiled my great plan—or would if horses were not too stupid to think—well, I shall deal with him too, and not gently!

Editor's Note: Ugh! We apologize heartily for subjecting your sensitive eyes and delicate, discerning minds to such a revolting manifesto as the above, but some on our editorial board argue that it is better to know what this repulsive individual is up to than to stick our noses in the air and remain ignorant.

WE PROTEST!
THE CHARACTERS OF

THE *BOOK* OF *SQUIDLY LIGHT*
SPEAK OUT

(Grumbling voice heard off stage:
"That cat gets all the attention!")

Enough is enough, in fact it's too much, and the time has come to speak! Cats are all very well in their way... well they *may* be all very well, though not all of us necessarily *like* cats...

But the encroachments of one F. Atty. Lumpkin, Attorney at Law, have become unbearable to the rest of us. After all, he is merely an unnamed and infinitely minor character in *The Way Beyond*, and though his role in *The Book of Squidly Light* is far greater, even there he is merely one of five or ten major characters. Yet on the Delirious Walrus website, he has two or three whole sections to himself, while the rest of us have nothing! And we understand that even in this short compendium, he has a whole separate section. It's absurd!

After intense collective bargaining with the web developers, editors, and imaginary author Karima Vargas Bushnell—you didn't think she was real, did you?—we have been given this venue to air our grievances and share our genius. For there *are* geniuses among us. Not *all* of us maybe...

Shut up, Basel. And we have been silent too long.

Signed,
 Basel Vasselschnauzer,
 Sophie McGregor,
 Muhammad Abdurraheem Hussayn*,
 Squidress Four,
 the Nanobots,
 and a Certain Horse.
 Halycon Sage abstains.

(Voices heard offstage: "Fatty Lumpkin is my friend and I love him and he's worth all of them put together! "That's alright, Nuri, the great ones always arouse some jealousy".)

---

*Somebody talked Abdurraheem into signing this. It's not like him at all.

PART FIVE

F. Atty Lumpkin Esq.

A CAT-ATTORNEY CALLED TO THE BAR[1]

Editor's Note:

Fatty Lumpkin appears as a bit player in *The Way Beyond* and a major character in *The Book of Squidly Light*. His educational addresses and historically accurate tales which follow are supplementary to the books, but with Fatty's discovery of The Black Foam Ball of Ultimate Significance, fantasy and reality impinge upon each other.

---

1. Yes, I know that some of you have also been "called to the bar," but this is not like that. This is something entirely different. —F. Atty. Lumpkin, Esq.

AN IMPORTANT MESSAGE

FROM THE DESK OF F. ATTY LUMPKIN
RE: MEERKATS!

F. LUMPKIN. Friends, it has come to my attention that there is a creature, a warm-blooded mammal, currently being referred to as a meerkat.[1] I must protest the describing of any creature as a mere cat! While this animal is obviously inferior to the true cat—its stance oddly humanesque, its ears too rounded, and its expression somewhat vacant, thought its tail is quite pleasing—still, it is obviously *some* sort of cat, otherwise why the name?

This has come to my attention, and I must protest. I am herewith filing an ORDER TO CEASE AND DESIST, A WRIT OF MANDAMUS, A BILL OF ATTAINDER AND A BILL OF LADING. The individuals or groups using this term, to wit, "meerkat" or "mere cat" must CEASE AND DESIST immediately! Or somebody might leave a little present on your pillow. Because we all know that the Cat is a most extraordinary and admirable animal, and that a cat, no matter how oddly shaped, can never be "mere".

Thank you.

---

1. Photos of this animal are easily viewable if you are in a dimension with internet capabilities.

A Note from
The Book of Squidly Light Publication Team:

We on *The Book of Squidly Light* Publication Team have received a comment from an anonymous dog.

Feeling that the Cat Fatty Lumpkin (deceased) is the best one to handle this inquiry, which is not precisely relevant to what we are doing, we have turned the matter over to him.

The next chapter contains a record of correspondence related to this matter, transcribed for your edification and enjoyment.

WHY ARE

THERE NO "DOGAGORIES"?

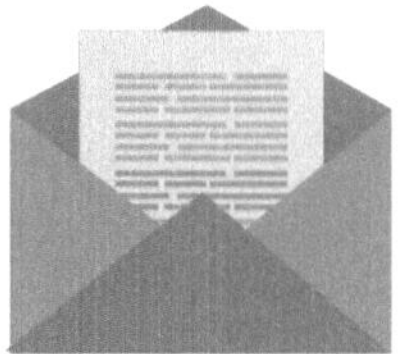

from: **The Book Of Squidly Light Publication Team**
<SquidTeam@DeliriousWalrus.com>
to: **Fatty Lumpkin ESQ**
<F.ATTYLUMPKINESQ@DeliriousWalrus.com>
subject: FWD: This is a dog-gone OUTRAGE!

Fatty
Please find attached a comment from an anonymous dog which needs
attention. We feel that you are the best suited to respond to this matter.

Thank you,
The Book of Squidly Light Publication Team

---------- Forwarded message ----------
from: **Anonymous Dog**
<email hidden>
to: **The Book Of Squidly Light Publication Team**
<SquidTeam@DeliriousWalrus.com>
subject: This is a dog-gone OUTRAGE!

To Whom it May Concern,

Why Are There No "Dogagories?" I Protest!

Signed,
 Anonymous Dog

***

from: **Fatty Lumpkin ESQ**
<F.ATTYLUMPKINESQ@DeliriousWalrus.com>
to:**The Book Of Squidly Light Publication Team**
<SquidTeam@DeliriousWalrus.com>
subject: Re: FWD: This is a dog-gone OUTRAGE!

Dear Squidly Light Team,

What needs attention, the comment or the dog? Please be more specific.

If some Earth-dog needs my attention, I would gladly arrange a mind-meld to provide encouragement, motivation or advice. But if it's a question of food, water, walks, etc., I am incorporeal and cannot help.

I cannot address these complex legal questions unless I am given full information.

Sincerely,
F. Atty. Lumpkin

from: **The Book Of Squidly Light Publication Team**
<SquidTeam@DeliriousWalrus.com>
to: **Fatty Lumpkin ESQ**
<F.ATTYLUMPKINESQ@DeliriousWalrus.com>
subject: Re: FWD: This is a dog-gone OUTRAGE!

Dear Fatty,

With all due respect, we believe you are quite aware that it is the question, not the dog, that needs your attention. We would appreciate a response at your earliest convenience.

Regards,
The Book of Squidly Light Publication Team

***

from: **Fatty Lumpkin ESQ**
<F.ATTYLUMPKINESQ@DeliriousWalrus.com>
to: **Anonymous Dog**
<email hidden>
subject: Dogagories would be a catastrophe

Dear Dog,

You are outraged by the lack of dogagories but in all the annals of world religions, you will find no mention of "Catma"! This cuts both ways, my canine friend!

Regards,
F. Atty Lumpkins Esq. (*deceased*)

from: **Anonymous Reader**
<email hidden>
to: **The Book Of Squidly Light Publication Team**
<SquidTeam@DeliriousWalrus.com>
subject: Fact Check

To the Editors at the Squidly Light Team,

How does the cat type if he has no thumbs? He isn't some strange new thumbed cat, is he?

Signed,
 Anonymous Reader

***

from: **The Book Of Squidly Light Publication Team**
<SquidTeam@DeliriousWalrus.com>
to: **Anonymous Reader**
<email hidden>
subject: RE: Fact Check

Reader,

Please pay closer attention. This cat has migrated to the Spirit World. He does it with his mind, of course!

Respectfully,
The Book of Squidly Light Publication Team[1]

------

1. You can direct questions and comments to Sage, Karima, or various characters by scanning the QR code or visiting the web address below. We'd be delighted to hear from you.

   https://DeliriousWalrus.com/reader-request/

THE LUMPKIN DIARIES:

Chronicles ^{of the} Cat F. Atty Lumpkin, Esq.

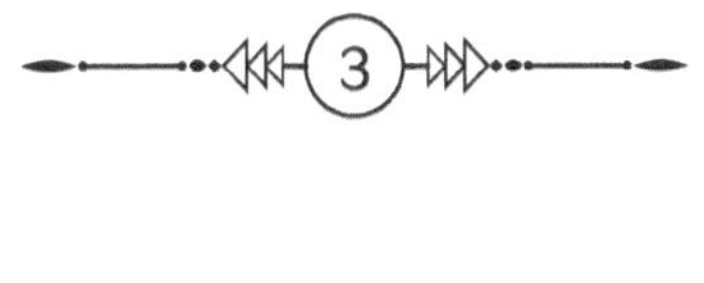

Prologue

If you know *The Book of Squidly Light*, you may know that the Cat Fatty Lumpkin is on record as lamenting his regrettable Lack of Thumbs, and also that he kept a diary which only one other character had been privileged to see. The next person to encounter this interesting document was Karima, his human companion in the Alternate Universe, who found it during Fatty's Mysterious Illness, at which time she took the pen from his failing paw and continued the narrative in his place.

So far we have protected his privacy, but due to the apocalypsish peculiarities of our post-modern times, some new publishing realities, and the prevalence of zombies—well, we only know of one, but he is pretty frickin' prevalent—we are herewith, heretofore, hereby, and forthwith publishing *The Lumpkin Diaries*. His adventures recounted here happened in real life, exactly as described.

The present document includes records of his daily activities, advice and personal revelations to his heart-friend Radar the Turkish Wondercat, sections written by Karima as described above, and explanatory interpolations by ourselves, the Editors and/or the Squidly Light Editorial Team.

Fatty began his diary out of frustration at becoming an indoor cat, though in a new larger house where there was fine window access. While Karima (a.k.a. Mother) regretted his distress, it was really just too dangerous out there, to Fatty, to various birds, and to one chipmunk! A beloved elderly neighbor used to inquire hopefully whether he was still alive (hoping *not,* as he made a habit of sitting under her bird feeder). But Fatty had the last laugh: When she died peacefuly well into her 90s, he was still around.

Finally, none of this will avail if The Red Chair of Death has been placed in front of the fridge.

From F. Atty Lumpkin,
The Lumpkin Diaries;
Part One, The Daring Raids.

THE LUMPKIN DIARIES:

THE DARING RAIDS

11.10.13. *The Lumpkin Diaries* begin. Time 10.11 hours, weather N. by S.W., cold, no wind. Successful raid on highest cupboard last night. Technique has improved: was able to dine in place without knocking 17.6-lb bag of cat food to floor. Mother's attempt to close bag with chip-clip unsuccessful. We are gaining and collating new knowledge all the time. FYI, dear Radar Love Felinestein.

[Editor's Note: This International Cat of Mystery was Fatty's closest online companion during their time on earth and plays an intimate, though physically distant, part in his adventures.]

12.13.13. Radar Love Felinestein, this is Fatty Lumpkin. You asked me quite a while ago how to get into the refrigerator. Please excuse the discourtesy of such a belated reply. The procedure is simple. You simply insert your paw in the crack under the door (or, if facing a side-by-side, your nose in the crack between fridge and freezer) and pull or push. This method may also be applied to cabinet doors with good effect. Even if your fridge doors are too tight for this, the humans are sometimes careless and close them imperfectly. You can make a patrol several times a day to see if this has happened. I do. Finally, none of this will avail if The Red Chair of Death has been placed in front of the fridge. But you can sit on it while contemplating your next move. A word of cheer: The humans always slip up eventually. I got some turkey the other night.

Undated. Weather cloudy, wind indeterminate. The humans made a turkey in a roasting pan, placing the leftovers in the refrigerator. Mother put the Red Chair of Death against the fridge door, precluding entry. But that was where they made their mistake. Mother washed the roasting pan, then left it on the Red Chair for some taller person to return to the high shelf. *And I went and sat in it!* Guess I scotched *that* little plan! At least she had to wash it again to pay for all my trouble.

8.28.14. I snagged most of a free-range salami for myself and my brothers from the fridge this morning. We did not appear for breakfast, as we did not require any little kibble bits.

9.8.14. 13:00. Declined invitation to breakfast. Mom: I *know* I put the chair back in front of the fridge! Dad: Yeah, while you were away, he learned to move the chair—I put *two* chairs now.
1/2 order roast turkey, dressing, mashed potato, gravy. Also 1/2 steak and fried onions. Tasted nice.

—F. Lumpkin

9.19.14. Weather variable, Time whatever. Dear Diary, only in your kindly pages would I disclose what I am about to say. So glad I have you to talk to, Diary! Okay, here it is: Though I am a most dominant and daring cat in the areas of food-stealing and sneaking outdoors—an example for all cats to follow—for some reason sleeping spaces are different. My brother Venchy is pulling his 'corporate takeover' act again. He sits on the strategic corner of the big bed at night and tells me, "Karima is MY mommy, NOT your mommy! You can't be in here, you have to go away!" And to my shame, I do. I skulk away and sit at the bottom of the stairs wearing my sad-old-man face. If Karima figures out this has happened, she comes and gets me, but still…Diary, I'm so glad I have you to confide in, as I would not want anyone else to know.

—F. Lumpkin (a.k.a. Benjamin Felinus)

THE LUMPKIN DIARIES:

Fatty's Mysterious Illness

5.24.15. To Radar the Turkish Wondercat a.k.a. International Cat of Mystery:

Many happy returns of the day, Good Sir!

I must unburden my heart to you regarding a Certain Matter: My brother Venchy Cat is getting all the attention! They are always fussing over him, and he gets pills, subcutaneous water, special food...Do *I* get any of these things? No! It puts me in mind of the Biblical quote where somebody complains to his father, "You never gave ME a fatted calf that I might make merry with my friends!" No, they didn't. They did not even give me a chicken wing.

Yours, with kind regards but in some disgruntlement,

—F. Lumpkin

[Editor's Note: Be careful what you wish for!!!]

[Karima's Note: Believe me, Lumpkin, you wouldn't like it if you had it!]

[Editor's Note: Though Karima had been posting about Fatty Lumpkin for quite some time in the Alternate Universe, where you, Dear Reader, doubtless live, it was not until this trying time that she found his text and realized that he had been keeping a record of his own. Fatty being incapacitated due to the above-referenced illness, Karima was afforded much comfort and relief by taking pen in hand and continuing his Chronicle, as he surely would have wished.]

7.25.15. Dears, Fatty Lumpkin has some kind of crazy brain/neurological thing and is at the university veterinary hospital right now (went in last night) with an M.R.I. scheduled for 1:00 p.m. He's as nice and wonderful a cat as ever lived; your prayers and good thoughts would be much appreciated. My impression is that this could go either way.

Written later. The next two days were terrifying for those who loved Fatty Lumpkin. He not only stopped eating, but spent time sitting in a corner staring blankly at the wall, did not respond to any overture from us or the other cats, and was totally without affect. A creature less like the loving, witty, self-determined, and adventurous cat we knew could not be imagined! A vet at University of Minnesota emergency who did not know him asked, "Is this cat normally unengaged?" We were torn between outrage and hysterical laughter. But, Dear Reader, we will not prolong your agony of suspense.

7.26.15. Fatty Lumpkin is okay!! Long story, but we had to run to the U of M emergency vet again last night. He had oxygen, stayed over, and is now absolutely back to his normal self—loving, feisty and brilliant. They're baffled. He apparently poisoned himself somehow, but we may never know what it was.

Undated. Fatty had a terrible relapse, without the loss of affect but with a complete inability to eat or drink, as though he had forgotten even how to lap water. He did learn to signal us when he was thirsty. (By a look in the eyes? Some sound or movement? Filling in blank spots in this diary years later, I forget how he did it, but it was the equivalent of a paralyzed patient communicating by twitching one eye lid.) But read on.

8.29.15. Fatty Lumpkin ate something!!! I drove to the Dances of Universal Peace retreat at 4:00 this morning (Note to self: don't do that, you can't see signs in the dark), came home, and petted him on the porch swing for about 20 minutes. His red, toast, and marshmallow colored fur was so beautiful in the sun, and his neck fur glistened like metallic gold, it really did. And then he ate almost a whole slice of roast turkey. The Cat Who Forgot How to Eat may have a happy ending after all.

RETURN TO ORIGINAL AUTHORSHIP

[Editors Note: The Lumpkin Diaries Resume! The real diaries, we mean, not the well meaning but obviously inferior interpolations contributed by his human friend Karima (a.k.a. Mother). It is best when a cat speaks for himself!]

9.10.15. 0900 hours. Latitude diffuse, weather variable. Tonight I awakened from a dazed state, possibly induced by some plot on the part of the humans. I have vague memories of being fed turkey baby food through a syringe and believe this continued for several weeks or months. In front of me on the bed was a plate of Mother's taco fixings, including some browned ground turkey, of which Mother is fond. I ate it. She did not appear to notice, being absorbed in *Grey's Anatomy*. To repeat, I ate it. It was almost too easy.

—F. Lumpkin

10.7.15. "I still got it!" – Jimmy Durante. "Yeah, baby!" – Austin Powers. My Mommy came downstairs just now to make tea and found (a) the refrigerator door wide open, (b) a package of tomatoes upside down on the kitchen floor and (c) (Score!) a package of kosher beef hotdogs on the dining room rug. Slightly opened and eaten, bearing evidence of "tooth and claw". And I looked at her with such innocent eyes!

—Yours truly,
F. Atty. Lumpkin

THE LUMPKIN DIARIES:

THROUGH THE BINOCULAR GAZE OF CAT AND HUMAN

[Editor's Note: Since the following entries come about equally from both parties, we are identifying them simply as FATTY and KARIMA. He has still signed some entries, because he likes to.]

Karima Vargas Bushnell, Alternate Universe "owner" of the Cat Fatty Lumpkin, was remembering that she had gotten his name from the Tolkien book, though she did not remember quite how or why. The imaginary author wondered why such an elegant creature should be stuck with such a stupid name.

One day it came to her: The cat was an *attorney!* He was F. Atty. Lumpkin, Esq. Now it all made sense: his style, his behavior, the charming way he communicated with her, mostly getting her to do whatever he wanted while making her feel that he was doing her a favor.

12.20.15. KARIMA. Cat notes. When Fatty Lumpkin wants to come into the bedroom and the door is closed, he stands up and manipulates the doorknob back and forth to make the sound of someone trying to get in. (In the old house, he slid his paw under the door and moved it back and forth very fast, simulating the sound of the FBI initiating a raid.) Bob remains Bob. He's sleeping in my spot, but I have worked hard and deserve a nap. I intend to move him.

12.30.15. KARIMA. Interesting new sensation this morning: cat chewing on my head while down in *sajda* (prostrating prayer position). Bob, not Lumpkin.

1.7.16. FATTY. Friends, thank you for your kind inquiries. I am well, but have been undercover for periods of time, so have been communicating less than usual. It is hard to communicate through all those blankets.

– F. Lumpkin, a.k.a., F. Atty. Lumpkin, Esq.

1.14.16. KARIMA. Some website says that there are three kinds of cats: Those who don't realize things can be changed, those who know that *you* (humans) can change things, and those who change things for themselves. That's one reason I love Fatty Lumpkin so much: He's incredibly proactive!

1.18.16. KARIMA. Fatty Lumpkin did not attend breakfast this morning. Fridge door was open, some beef baloney on the dining room rug, satisfied cat sleeping on bed. Bob had breakfast as usual, so apparently did not share in the feast.

6.6.16. FATTY. Radar, my friend, what's this I hear about you not eating? Would you not reconsider? You know my spies are everywhere.

Signed,
F. Atty Lumpkin, Attorney at Law
and Orange Traditional Tabby

7.11.16. FATTY. I'm playing! I'm playing! I have a magnificent new toy; Mom calls it a 'roll of paper towels'! I have not played like this since I was a kitten, and maybe not then. A whole new world is opening up...

—F. Lumpkin, Esq.
(a Feline American)

10.08.16. FATTY. Meerkats! I have just heard about the pressing issue of meerkats. I must write about this and let everyone know.

12.08.16. KARIMA. Fatty Lumpkin has a toy! He has never been one for physical possessions—not like his Brother Venchy, who liked to play fetch with a plastic bottle cap—but now Fatty has a black foam microphone cover[1] that he hauls around and sometimes brings to me in triumph, with breathless anticipation, like Paul Revere delivering a message. He doesn't want to fetch it though. I think he plays English football with it.

12.13.16. KARIMA There is a cat IQ test at Kinko's and I'm tempted to test our feline attorney, cracksman, and escape artist, F. Atty. Lumpkin, Esq. (I never did. What a pity.)

12.23.16. KARIMA. Ok, this is weird. If you're following the adventures of Fatty Lumpkin, you know that he has a new toy he carries everywhere, to wit, a black foam microphone cover, which he believes will solve humanity's problems. Now some of you may think I'm writing Fatty's posts, and maybe I thought so too. But after Fatty described his new possession, his online friend Radar the Turkish Wondercat wrote, "I want one! Do you have two?" Fatty replied that he would check into it and report back soon. All normal so far, right? But in the weeks that he has been carrying this around, we've never seen him with more than one. The next day after the conversation, suddenly there were two. This cat really is a genius. Is there something going in here that I don't know about?

12.23.16. KARIMA. My nephew has informed me that the law degree was from Kitten University. I'm not sure how F. Atty. attended classes. Maybe it's a correspondence school.

---

1. To find out more about The Black Foam Ball of Ultimate Significance and its role in a gallant attempt to save Planet Earth (and maybe the whole multiverse), see *The Book of Squidly Light.*

FROM

THE CAT MAFIA

Fatty Lumpkin has decided he should be fed in the middle of every night, and has instituted Pavlovian training to that effect. Polite requests such as waking the subject/minion (me) with a direct look in the eyes and a pointed meow having failed, and there being no bell pull available, Fatty has instituted creative methods. The first go-to is walking around on the two dressers. Since their surfaces are covered with clutter as well as an old-fashioned lamp, the threat of knocking everything to the floor provides considerable motivation. This method has a distinct Mafia quality. "You certainly have some beautiful *things* on your dressers, some *breakable*. It would be a shame if anything *happened* to them." If this fails, moving and rattling the large, heavily framed picture directly above the sleeper's head, presaging the possible precipitation of said picture onto said head, has provided a hitherto irresistible motivation.

I see that, in writing about F. Atty. Lumpkin, Esq., I have inadvertently adopted his style. Taking the pen [or keyboard] kindly but firmly from The Author, F. Atty. Lumpkin continues, wishing that if this story be told, it be told right. Fatty continues:

At this point in the nightly dance, I subtly introduce the idea into the subject's mind that, once she is downstairs to feed me, there can be a cup of tea. My method of doing this is classified. My late lamented friend,

Radar the Turkish Wondercat, would have understood. Night before last, for the first time ever, these methods failed for a simple reason I had not anticipated and could not have controlled; we were out of milk! The subject remained firmly in bed, refusing all threats and blandishments, adding the indignity of putting me outside the door (twice). Not wishing to lose the effect of weeks of training, I stepped in her ear. Unfortunately, and accidentally, one of my claws was out, precipitating a loud howl from the subject and drawing first blood in this, our battle of wills. The error is deeply regretted. Also regretted is the fact that she never did get out of bed to feed me.

POSTSCRIPT

^{ON} FATTY LUMPKIN

In describing Fatty through two novels and a diary, I see that I have emphasized his cleverness at the expense of his sweetness, which balanced it all and made him like a fine wine with complex flavors. (Except, a cat, though. You would not want to drink a cat, as it would be too furry for your throat.)

Fatty was one of four tabby kittens born to a queen[1] from an apple farm. In the daytime, the five-cat family would sleep in two-, three-, and four-cat piles, fitted together like a patchwork quilt. At night, Fatty's brother Venchy slept on top of us, while Fatty slept under the covers with part of his orange face peeking out. Thus we called them the mountain cat and the cave cat. (This is also why he was "an undercover cat", which appellation adds to his spy-like mystique.)

Their brother Bob, a calm, benign, luxuriantly-furred armful weighing 19 pounds, was voted Cat Most Frequently Mistaken for Laundry. There are other feline-related benefits to being nearsighted: Besides the laundry thing, the cursive writing on our old-fashioned faucets appeared to me, without glasses, to say "Hot and Cats". I used to picture a stream of tiny cats running out of the cold tap.

---

1. A queen is a mother cat, in case you didn't know.

When Venchy was 15 and his time came to join The Great Cat in The Sky, we called Fatty over to see the body. This might sound shocking, but it isn't good for an animal to keep wondering where their friend is. (In our family, we refer to such a body as "a cat sock," because the actual cat has obviously left.)

Fatty leaped down from the cat-furniture crow's nest in his usual dashing way to see what was up. There was a long moment while he stood and looked and realized. Then the wind went out of his sails and he became, in a moment, an *old* cat. He and the ever-reliable Bob lay curved around Venchy for two hours. We gave them their time.

Years later when Fatty's turn came to move on, as we all must do, he had grown weak and exhausted. Yet the night before his passing, he suddenly gathered his strength, stood up, and almost ran to me from where he lay on the other side of the big bed, landing with a thump against my chest. We lay like that for hours.

My religion says, "You will be with those you love." I am holding them to that!

PART SIX

From the Green World to the World of Light

ON ^{THE} BRIGHT,

LUMINOUS, FLASHING SIDE ...

"Halycon Sage was life, simplicity, Reality, the breath
of mystery—the thing we all believe in before we don't.
That was Halycon Sage."

—*The Way Beyond,*
chap. 19, para. 48

So, here's the good news: The doors and portals, Aladdin's Cave
(with far better jewels than rubies and diamonds), the sign "For
Madmen Only" that appears and disappears on the alley wall—
they're all real. Perhaps not in detail, but in essence. And the quest to
find them is real too, and anyone deeply willing can go. We all know the
requisites: courage, determination, and the ability to last through deserts
of boredom, high ocean waves of fear, and distracting tropical islands of
temptation to false trails and bad values. (No worries, though, because
they also lead to deserts of awe-filled silence, oceans of love and mercy,
and tropical islands of infinitely profuse and detailed beauty.) Also
required: imagination, the ability to throw off the dull, banal, deadening
enchantment that says there is no sun, but only a lamp in a dungeon,

made sun by your self-delusion.[1] So, the eternal call is sounding, the leap is there to be taken. There are a thousand, million doors and portals that work—just choose what the possibly mythical Don Juan Matus called "a path with heart". This has been a public service announcement from the Friends of the Unseen, protectors of Halycon Sage and his author.

____

1. C.S. Lewis, *The Silver Chair*

TOM BOMBADIL,

*"Tom was here before the river and the trees...He made
paths before the Big People, and saw the Little People arriving...
When the Elves passed westward, Tom was already here, before
the seas were bent...before the Dark Lord came from Outside."* [1]

TOM BOMBADIL! Sound familiar? Or if not, how about *The Lord of
the Rings*? Tom was in the books, but didn't make it into the movies.
"What does this have to do with *The Book of Squidly Light?*" you ask.
A lot.

Tom Bombadil lives in the Old Forest with his wife Goldberry.
Entwined with nature, full of joy, always singing. Inconceivably ancient,
he goes about his business unaffected by humans, elves, dwarves or
hobbits, though he sometimes helps if needed. The One Ring, symbol
of ultimate power which fills everyone else with fear or desire, means
nothing to him.

Tom is a friend of nature and the earth, perhaps a personification

---

1. Tom Bombadil describing himself in J.R.R. Tolkien's *The Fellowship of
the Ring.*

of them, and he's a friend of the Ents, the great, wise, slow-moving and utterly convincing tree people. (Those who think tree hugging is funny haven't done it right. Each tree is different; you can feel this if you try.)

"C'mon!" you say impatiently (unless you love Tom Bombadil), "There are no *Squid* in this!"

Alright, alright, I'm getting to it. Tom has a string of ponies. The lead pony—the wisest, cleverest, most magical of them all—is called Fatty Lumpkin. And the anonymous orange cat from *The Way Beyond*, stepping up as a major character in *The Book of Squidly Light*, is his namesake: Fatty Lumpkin, as clever a cat as ever walked the Earth Plane.

If this isn't a close enough connection for you, Tom would be *down* with our characters' core mission of saving the lovely Planet Earth. We're all on the same side here. Except for a couple of villains.

STAY CLOSE

There Was or There Was Not (that's a version of Once Upon a Time) a town that was threatened by an invading enemy. Because the enemy had an army of sleepwalkers, though they fought fiercely and believed themselves awake, there was no possibility of making friends with them. The people of the town could not run away, and they could not fight back. Never mind why. At this particular time and place, they had only two choices, with, perhaps, an intermediate, wishy-washy choice in the middle.

They had been told by a Wise Being that they could survive if they fortified their town and waited out the coming attack. There was plenty of food within the town, as the people had been preserving and storing part of their harvest for many years, but there was a problem about water—it was running out. They had a Very Special Water Tank, light as a feather and perhaps with magical properties, that could store what they needed if only they had the water in the first place. But someone had to go and get it from the Huge Deep Lake.

The tasks that needed doing in preparation for the siege were few and specific: to build higher the mud brick wall around the town, and to go for water. Building the wall higher meant first gathering reeds and mud from the little pond just outside the city gates, which had enough water to make the mud, but not enough for thirsty people under siege, then molding and forming the bricks, then stacking them higher. All these tasks were done in groups, working with family and friends, staying close within the community.

But going for the water had to be done alone. The Very Special Water Tank only worked in the presence of one person. With two, it was heavy as lead. One villager—we'll call her Shayda, which might not mean anything—had been trained from birth in the intricate ways of reaching the Huge Deep Lake, coaxing the water into the tank, and returning safely. Specific knowledge was needed for this, as the Lake was difficult to find, being down a winding path and sometimes invisible. A certain frame of mind was needed to access the water, and the ways both forward and back were filled with distractions.

Shayda's problem was that she knew how to reach the water (sometimes) and bring it back (God willing!) but she didn't want to leave the people. She felt that they needed her, that every pair of hands should work to make the bricks, and that the path to the Huge Deep Lake was lonely. And boring! And that thinking she should forget the bricks and concentrate on the water might be escapist, or elitist, or some kind of ist, anyway. Only the first part of the path was lonely, the rest was filled with delightful sights, sounds, adventures and companionships, but she could never remember this. She wanted to stay with the people, and help, and be two hands among the many, working in harmony.

She wasn't the only one trained in the water-fetching. In fact, some souls further along in their training lived out in the wilderness beside the path and sometimes delivered water to the village by their own methods. Still, not too many were trained and tested in the water gathering, and she was one. She had had an Excellent Teacher.

So we leave this story, perhaps to return to it sometime, perhaps not. There were only two choices, with, perhaps, an intermediate, wishy-washy choice in the middle. The intermediate, wishy-washy choice was gathering just a little water from the pools that lined the near part of the path and bringing it back: a journey less lonely and more quickly accomplished. And each villager must make this choice, and make it again and again every day. Some live in solitude far along the Waterward Path, while others are experts in brick making and wall building, and for them the choice is easier than for those of us who fall in the middle. And on this day, Shayda made the wishy-washy choice, which is why she is bringing you this story.

The End

REPARATIONS FOR THE ANIMALS

(ᴬ Lᴇɢᴀʟ Dᴏᴄᴜᴍᴇɴᴛ)

IN THE MATTER OF:
ANIMALS OF EARTH
vs.
PERCEIVED UNFAIRNESS OF THE UNIVERSE

Attorney of Record: F. Atty. Lumpkin, Esq., a Feline American

COMPLAINT

COME NOW THE PLAINTIFFS, F. Atty. Lumpkin, Esq., Cat-Attorney Called to the Bar, and Associates No-Name Stupid, Horse Extraordinaire and Poet, and Karima Vargas Bushnell, Animal Empath, asking Compensation and Reparations for the Animals.

OH ONE WITHOUT A SECOND:
OF YOUR POWER, we demand relief and compensation, with full consideration of pain and suffering, for the farm animals, the laboratory animals, the victims of habitat loss, of abandonment, of things too painful to describe even here, in this most serious Complaint.

BEFORE YOUR LOVE, Oh Compassionate and Merciful, we bring the case of these Little Ones. Knowing that Your physical reality—this Persian carpet, this Chinese puzzle box—cannot accommodate our request,

NOW THEREFORE, we pray for their Relief, Compensation, and Blessing outside and beyond this earthly life, including but not limited to

LOVE AND DELIGHT: Care, nurture and compassion; petting and play; reunion with friends, companions, offspring and mates; warm hugs, sweet tears on their fur for such as would like them. Silence and whale song and bird song. The grace of cold or heat or water, whatever is most pleasing, upon their fins and scales, upon their snouts and claws. Romping through fields, sleeping in sun or shade, or curled in furry piles of boon companions. Leaping through oceans. For the predator, wild intrepid hunting. Glaciers beyond measure, or jungles thick and deep, whatever is their pleasure. Dark burrows filled with worms to eat, with no pain to the worms themselves. Infinite skies to fly in, great nests for their welcome home.

APPRECIATION: To know that they are wondrous and adored, their beauty or fierceness or humor *seen*, immeasurable contribution to the tapestry of life, loved by many, many, many of their fellow creatures, and most of all, by You. And that we aspire to love them as they are, not as we imagine them to be.

EVOLUTION: For those who wish, higher levels, new insight and knowledge, a Light to their intelligence: lizard to dragon, parrot to phoenix. For those who wish, a dancing with Your angels, a conscious journey toward Your Nearness.

WE PLEAD, PRAY, AND DEMAND, of Your Justice and Compassion, all this and more, since what we conceive for them is the groping of a blind mouse in a dark tunnel, the philosophy of a microbe, against Your Love and Knowledge, Secret Beloved, Nearest of the Near.

YOU KNOW AND WE DO NOT KNOW, but of Your Justice and Compassion, we humbly request this Relief and Compensation for all the Animals.

SETTING OUR PAW, HAND, HOOF, AND SEAL
to this document in all Sincerity and Respect
2023 A.D. / 1445 A.H.

F. Atty. Lumpkin, Esq.,
Discarnate Cat-Attorney at Large in the Multiverse
Assisted by No-Name Stupid, a Horse of Great Resources
Karima Bushnell, Secretary

Amin. So may it be.

P.S. And for the trees, too!

COMMITTEE MEETING

CHAIN REACTIONS

WARNING:
The following does not claim to be an accurate representation
of the Higher Planes or What's Really Going On if We Only Knew.
The idea came to the author while changing a cat box at 4 a.m.
It is what it is, baby.

The Muslim Council overseeing its constituents on Earth from the Higher Planes was in session. Things were not going well down there. Three dimensions down, four up, and seven over, the Christian and Hindu Councils were each having their own meetings. Things were not going well for them either, but that is not our concern at the moment.

Of course, the One Who Can Never Be Adequately Described (not by a billionth of a billionth of a nano-particle) was really performing every action and present to all, but the committees did not know this.

Though they subscribed to this doctrine in theory and understood it when they became immersed in the Presence—when that happened they laughed and cried etherically and their joy poured down on the Earth, giving everyone a good day—like many on the planet itself, they were unable to sustain the realization. Since their names are of no concern to us here, though you might be familiar with some of them from the mystical literature, we'll give them generic designations.

SOMEONE. We've made a complete mess. Again.

ANOTHER. Look at them down there! They're insulting and killing each other over anything and nothing. They're crazy!

ANOTHER OTHER. Well, it's not *their* fault. They're so frustrated, like rats in a maze with no way through and no cheese at the end.

ANOTHER *Outraged.* There's plenty of cheese! Have you seen the multi-levelled paradises? And are you forgetting the Presence?

At the mention of the Presence (Whom they had momentarily forgotten), everybody remembered and melted into all-knowing bliss for a timeless time. That was what happened when you Remembered, even on Earth. Sweet rain filtering through sudden sunshine fell upon the land, delighting every heart. Squirrels and rabbits danced, and many humans felt a release, a lift in mood, a sudden inner sunshine. All the mystics laughed with joy. This was a chain reaction: Suddenly, they remembered too.

OTHER ONE *as the committee room reappeared.* So, we had that brilliant idea of constructing a society where everybody was told exactly what to do so they couldn't mess it up. "Do this, then do this, then do that." What time of day and how to wash first and the whole nine yards. Just spell it out, you said.

ANOTHER. Well, how was I to know they'd just resent it and end up barrelling through the prayers on automatic while thinking about lunch? We made it as simple as we could and they still blew it.

OTHER ONE. Yeah, genius, and the restrictions made them so mad that they took it out on each other, like that Earth story where the boss shames the employee and the employee goes home and yells at his wife and then she smacks the kid and the kid kicks the dog. Chain reaction.

ANOTHER OTHER. Why not a female employee and her *husband*? Your story is out of date.

Pause for semantic and inter-group wrangling.

ANOTHER. Okay, so the Christians and Hindus and Buddhists and Jews tried the same approach and it didn't work for them either. Just like us: about three out of a million people got enlightened, a few more got to hang out in green pastures eating fruit, and everybody else went nuts and started killing each other. Or as good as.

OTHER. You exaggerate.

ANOTHER. Exaggeration for emphasis. I *said,* "as good as."

ANOTHER OTHER. Okay, so we all agree that it didn't work. So, we tried the opposite. Just let everybody do whatever they want, see if they find the way naturally.

OTHER ONE *sarcastically.* Yeah, that was a great success. One big party, and just like with the first approach, a very few made it through, but most of them just made a mess. Everybody sleeping with everybody, then dumping them, taking every drug known to man, kids brought up by the TV, and don't get me started on materialism.

ANOTHER. "Greed is Good." Ecocide by mega-corporations and their crooked politicians.

ALL. Yeah!

Timeless pause of complete agreement. On earth, the Chain-Reaction Effect caused the creation of several viable Peace Processes and Ecology Working Plans. And the people having lunch had agreeable conversations with each other.

OTHER. So, telling them exactly what to do doesn't work, and letting them do whatever the hell they want doesn't work either. How about something in the middle?

PASSING CHRISTIAN COMMITTEE MEMBERS *In unison, overhearing as they come back from their own ethereal lunch.* Middle of the road Protestantism!

Pause.

MUSLIM COMMITTEE *sounding dispirited.* Yeah.

Long pause.

ANOTHER OTHER. Well, we'll have to try something else. Let's think.

It is possible that the committees are not quite as high up the chain of vibration as they think they are. Their continuing bureaucratic tendencies toward arguing and one-upmanship are distressing, but let us wish them well. They are doing the best they can.

The End

BILL ᵀᴴᴱ CAT

ᴬᴺᴰ ᵀᴴᴱ HOLY SPARKS

T he words cathect and cathexis are frustrating in the extreme because they have a wonderful meaning combined with a truly horrid sound. When my cat throws up, he inexplicably runs backwards, making the sounds of someone who has swallowed a fish bone. (If you read *The Book of Squidly Light*, you will understand more about the possible ramifications of such behavior, but never mind that now.) Remember Bill the Cat from Bloom County and the throwing-up-a-hairball noises he made?[1]

The word cathect, bringing to mind as it does various images of cat, aack! pthht! and ick! is not a word to be used lightly. But the *meaning* is quite lovely. Looking it up now…(time passes)… Oh. "Investment of mental or emotional energy in a person, object, or idea." Well, *that's* nothing to get excited about. I'd remembered this word as being much wider and richer: simply, the folding and binding of a beautiful, magical, and beloved person, thing, or idea into one's own identity, making them part of you. Further research needed…Okay, this was someone's attempt to translate *bezetsung*, German, "to hold or occupy". The commentator says that the subtleties of the word

---

1. Many fine pictures of Bill the Cat making these noises are available online.

were missed. For Freud, an "investment of libidinal energy," leading to all kinds of craziness. German through Freud into Latin into English. No wonder it's a mess!

In Jewish tradition, a calamity near the beginning of time called "The Shattering of the Vessels" scattered "the Holy Sparks" everywhere. The job of humanity is to gather them up. So we go through the world finding lost bits of light: in a face, a flower, an encounter, a piece of music. We make them part of us because they reflect our own souls. (Distortions include obsessive collecting of *things* and also trying to own people, but I'm not talking about that here.) Perhaps there is a better word for this, but there should at least be a prettier one.

In contrast, we have the word mellifluous: "Sweet-sounding, dulcet, honeyed, mellow, soft, liquid, silvery, soothing, rich, smooth, euphonious, harmonious, tuneful, musical." The word mellifluous is mellifluous. I *do* like congruity.

IMAGINARY AUTHOR

In mid-June of 2019, literary lion Halycon Sage wrote the following story about one of his characters, an imaginary author. While this is a work of fiction, in Sage's Alternate Universe it happened exactly as described.

Imaginary author Karima Vargas Bushnell has certain things in common with her creator, Halycon Sage, and one is a tendency to drag way too much stuff with her everywhere. Thus, she approaches the TSA security line in the Alternate Universe with:

- a rolling Widemouth Leather Underseat Carry On, this being a warm-buttery-brown miniature suitcase
- a newly purchased brushed-copper laptop computer
- a shiny, bright red violin case
- a little army-green purse crammed with everything else

The laptop was supposed to fit into a Special Slot on the side of the suitcase—the reason, other than its luxurious beauty, that the little suitcase had been purchased in the first place. The purse was supposed to occupy the interior of the case, along with a lot of other stuff. This worked as long as there was an elephant around to sit on it.

After minor misadventures and the usual juggling-act scramble with tickets and ID, our protagonist removes the laptop from the miniature suitcase (as per posted instructions), heaves the items into the white plastic baskets on the conveyor belt, and prepares to add the fiddle case.

AGENT. You can't go through here.

KARIMA. What do you mean, I can't go through here?

AGENT. Not with that. It's too long to fit in a basket.

Karima, momentarily bereft of speech, is unable to explain that she has put the fiddle case on the conveyor belt *without* a basket many times previously.

AGENT. You have to go down *there (indicating a lane by the far wall).*

KARIMA. But my stuff is already on *here.*

AGENT. It doesn't matter.

The imaginary author retires in defeat, leaving shoes, sweater, suitcase, laptop, lipstick, wallet, cards and ID in the hands of bored strangers, and dashes down to what turns out to be Lane Six, where the fiddle is put through without incident. Running back to her original Lane Whatever, she successfully recovers the items and hikes cheerily down a number of conveyor belts, this time for humans, in search of Gate G6.

(Approximately 15 minutes.)

Arriving there with a pleasing sense of triumph and ample time to catch her flight, she feels an icy chill down her back as she realizes that the coppery laptop is not in its special side slot.

It is gone.

Back she goes to Security, re-traversing the cavernous rooms containing the human conveyor belts. Hesitating to re-enter Security from the wrong side—forbidding signs say, "STOP!" "GO BACK!" and "DO NOT ENTER!"—she looks at the abandoned items above the various lanes. Nothing. Bravely she approaches an Official, explaining her separation from her Items and the whole sideshow.

OFFICIAL *(male, emotionally neutral).* Which lane did you come through?

KARIMA. I have no idea. One of these around here. Then they sent me to Lane Six.

OFFICIAL. Go and look at the lanes.

KARIMA. I already did, but I'll look again. *(She does. Nothing. She returns to the Official.)*

OFFICIAL *(after some checking around).* Well, it's not here. Did you come through South or North Security?

KARIMA *(hearing this distinction for the first time).* I have no idea. I think I was going south, so I must have come from the north. *(How she knew this she does not, as of this writing, remember.)*

OFFICIAL. Well, that's the other one. You should go back there.

KARIMA. Thank you.

(Approximately ten minutes.)

With a new official (female, friendlier), she goes through the whole dog and pony show again, explaining about the fiddle case, the baskets, her separation from her belongings, and the missing laptop.

NEW OFFICIAL. You can't have come through here, because we don't have that rule about the baskets.

KARIMA. Excuse me?

NEW OFFICIAL. If you'd come through here, you could have just put your violin on the conveyor belt.

Karima is once again speechless, and probably appears about to cry.

NEW OFFICIAL *(kindly)*. Go back to South again, you must have come through that one.

KARIMA. Thank you.

She goes. (*Approximately 10 minutes.*)

Back at South Security, she again approaches the Podium on High of the supervising Official. It's a new person. A nice looking but not excessively handsome tall young man with short hair and glasses. She explains the whole thing again, adding the latest adventures and the info about how she must have come through South. She shows him the Special Slot on the side of the Very Special Suitcase.

OFFICIAL *(gently)*. Have you looked inside?

KARIMA *(stunned, as if confronted with a problem in physics)*. What?

OFFICIAL *(gently)*. Have you looked inside?
  She does.
  There it is.

KARIMA. Oh ...

OFFICIAL. They're usually inside.

KARIMA. You are a genius!

OFFICIAL *(kindly).* I'm not a genius, I've just been here a while. Ninety-nine percent of the time, people put them inside. That's where they are.

Karima stands stunned. The author of *Autobiography of a Yogi* used a special phrase for the condition in which she now finds herself: "Like a cow staring at a train."

OFFICIAL *(very gently).* Would you like a hug?

The world stops and she considers, feeling no pressure, either inner or outer. The young man waits quietly. It is one of those timeless moments that seems to occupy either a long time or no time at all. She considers, calmly and objectively, whether or not she would like a hug.

"Yes, I would," says Karima.

There is a hug.

The End

Imaginary author Karima Vargas Bushnell would like to thank the underpaid, overworked, and underappreciated TSA officials for their kindness and compassion, especially the one at the end of this story. Or she would have liked to thank them, had she and they been real.

HOW I MET

Halycon Sage

It was in Reno a summer or two ago, next to the frozen food wall at one end of a supermarket on a golden afternoon. Best-friend-from-college Jeneane and I were picking up a few items.

There he was: Halycon Sage, the hero of my metafictional novels, hub and center of my world-building, whose writing career began, like mine, with hearing the dream words: "One-hundred-and-one Cows: A Novel".

I glanced again at his face, unobserved. Yes, it was definitely him. An Indian man picking out his groceries, maybe Paiute or Washoe, considering where we were. There was a quietness about him. Shorter than I'd imagined, and he'd aged a little, hair a bit gray, an added fullness to his face. Sage, ten or fifteen years after the first novel.

The aisle was empty except the three of us. I looked again, then walked quickly to my friend. She'd read the book.

"Look, it's Halycon Sage. See? Should I talk to him?"

"Yeah, go for it."

Did she and I even talk, or were there only gestures, a nod of the head, a shared eye-sparkle? You know how you communicate with someone you've known forever.

I needed to acknowledge him, but I didn't know how. Obviously I couldn't say, "Hello, you're my imaginary author that I made up."

Stepping up to him, I told my inner truth, lightly disguised in a form that made more sense.

"Excuse me, sir, I had to say hello to you. You really remind me of someone I knew a long time ago."

There was no questioning or challenging, no social embarrassment. He turned and looked at me, saw I was sincere and that it mattered a lot. Like Halycon Sage, he was so kind. Gentle, unhurried, a face full of experience and depth, full of knowledge and a deep courtesy.

He shook my held-out hand. We looked into each other's eyes and smiled. I don't know if he thought my treasured friend was dead or just swept from me by the winds of time, but he understood. Our words were soft and few.

Then we went our ways, having shared love, respect, and understanding. I think he knew how much it meant to me. And I will never forget him.

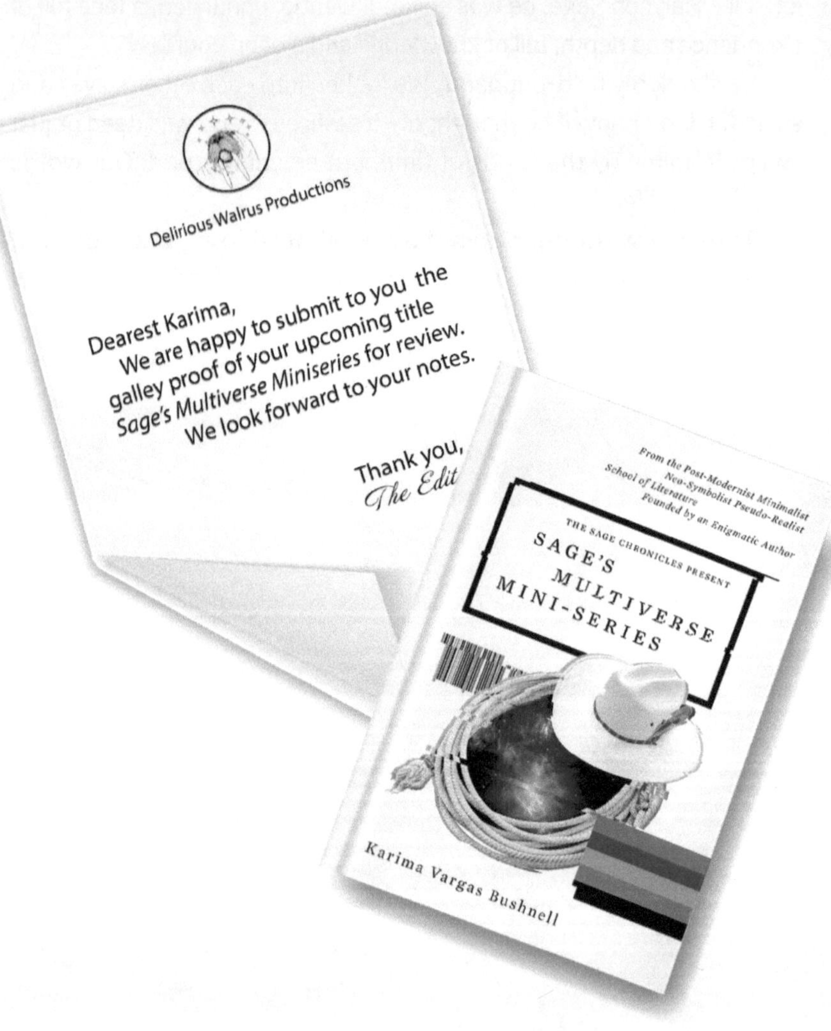
Delirious Walrus Productions

Dearest Karima,
We are happy to submit to you the
galley proof of your upcoming title
Sage's Multiverse Miniseries for review.
We look forward to your notes.

Thank you,
The Edit

From the Post-Modernist Minimalist
Neo-Symbolist Pseudo-Realist
School of Literature
Founded by an Enigmatic Author

THE SAGE CHRONICLES PRESENT
SAGE'S
MULTIVERSE
MINI-SERIES

Karima Vargas Bushnell

KID KARIMA

VS.

THE AUTHOR

KARIMA VARGAS BUSHNELL

Kid Karima

vs.

the Author

Karima Vargas Bushnell

*The new post-modernist minimalist neo-symbolist pseudo-realist inner monologue novel from world-famous Author Halycon Sage's protagnist Karima Vargas Bushnell
(Unless she's his creator: there is much debate over the matter.)*

KID KARIMA

vs. The Author

During the somewhat agonizing process of making final revisions to this first edition of *Sage's Multiverse Mini-Series*, I was forced to face the confusing fact that there are two of me. (Pronouns: she, her, and *sheesh*, sheesh being reserved for times when there is more than one of me in attendance.)

Upon first viewing the galley proof of the forthcoming book...

AUTHOR. *Oh...my...God.*

KID KARIMA. I love it, I love it, it's so *shiny*!

Author buries face in hands, just as Halycon Sage did when confronted with Deandra Hollendaise's mini-novel *Velveeta*.

KID KARIMA. And the colors! The *colors!*[1] *Magenta, turquoise, stars,* everything I *love!*

Author, face still buried in hands, begins rocking back and forth.

AUTHOR. This is a disaster. It's a *nightmare.* We're *ruined.*

KID KARIMA *(helplessly).* I *like* it.

Somewhere around this time the realization dawns upon Karima that her inner voices sound almost exactly like Pinkie and the Brain. A few moments pass while this stunning realization sinks in. Then the Karima-body currently occupied by these two opposing forces lifts sheesh's hand and opens the book. The type is HUGE! and in BOLD!

SAGE'S MULTIVERSE MINI-SERIES!

KID KARIMA *(staring in awe).* Whoa...

AUTHOR *(bending almost double, as if in actual pain).* Aaaargggh...

Author, somewhat more upright, begins thumbing through the text.

AUTHOR. These titles are *strange*. There's a disjunct. This huge upper title doesn't lead your attention to the lower, smaller, differently formatted subtitle. It's just kind of floating up there, and they don't seem related. Your eye doesn't track.

KID KARIMA. *Mine* does.

How can anyone have problems reading these titles and subtitles? she thinks. They are quite congenial to her kid/ADHD brain.

BOTH. And what about this free-floating question mark?

One likes it; the other thinks it's grotesque and pointless. They stare at each other helplessly. Now an interruption occurs. Suddenly, a voice shouts from a nearby room.

VOICE. *Dwarf spit!*

Karima responds happily, pleased at having her notions of reality confirmed.

KARIMA. *Dwarf spit!*

It's the plumber, conversing with Our Male Character, and he is obviously referring to some tool or esoteric plumbing matter, but both respond well to the echoed cry of Dwarf Spit, and jokes can be heard.[2]

AUTHOR. It looks like a kid's book. *(Shifting gaze from Book to Kid)* That's appropriate I suppose . . .

KID KARIMA. No, I don't *want* it to look like a kid's book!

AUTHOR. People would thumb through this and say, "It's a kids' book, I'm not interested."

(Author pauses, then unexpectedly offers a bit of hope.)

AUTHOR. It's *exuberant.* Exuberant is good. If you have that, it's much easier to rein it in than to go the other way . . .

KID KARIMA *(perking up).* Right, if was flat and boring, that would be much harder to fix!

KID KARIMA is nervous about discussing this with her book-publishing colleagues, because she has a near pathological fear of hurting anyone's feelings or making anyone mad at her. This only applies to those she cares about, but still, it's a problem, as her stylistic choices for speaking out are pathetic surrender versus Genghis Khan.

This is compounded by a second problem: While there are large areas of life (saving the Earth, anti-racism, chocolate) where she knows exactly what she thinks and can never be dissuaded, there's also a large, indeterminate area, a sort of gentle green valley between the mountains of the things she is sure about.

And in this green, quiet, neutral valley—which includes some aspects of the formatting of *Sage's Multiverse Mini-Series*—she genuinely agrees with whoever she is talking to.[3]

THE END

Notes

1. *Woah.* Is this a kid? Or some old acid freak? Or possibly both? Since psychedelics have apparently become respectable as a widespread therapeutic tool and the focus of such entities as Oregon's "Mommies on Mushrooms," there can be no harm in broaching the topic.

2. This Dwarf Spit thing happened, it really did. Though Karima discovered later that the men had thought she had said, "Horse spit!"

3. As long as the ideas are not stupid, which is a deal beaker.

FIVE FUN FACTS

Karima's lawyer father

was an expert rider, outdoorsman, and knew how to rope a calf. He used to announce the Reno rodeo, and one time as a kid she got to ride out into the arena with him in an open-air jeep.

The family took a cruise

to Hawaii when Karima was about five, and she hung out in the "oriental" gift shop on the ship. Her friend the proprietress told her, "I like your smile because it's real," and Karima wondered what other kind of smiles there could be.

At age 14, Karima and a friend held hands with

a long line of Green Bay Packers as they all ran into the warm, sunset-luminous ocean of Mazatlán, Mexico. It was the most fun ever!

Karima's parents were, respectively,

half German-Jewish and part Latino with a Native American component. Though she receives White Privilege and can 'pass', her heart and mind have always been a bit more global.

Karima loves animals with an aching passion,

and even though she's wary of spiders, she has a strange desire to see the World's Largest Tarantula Migration in Gabbs, Nevada.

AFTERWORD

Dᴇᴀʀ Rᴇᴀᴅᴇʀs, Tʜɪs Is Nᴏᴛ Gᴏᴏᴅʙʏᴇ

Karima's father, who would be 110 if he were alive today, used to tell the story of a boyhood visit to a traveling show that featured an optimistic man accompanied by a tired old hound dog. The star of the show lay unmoving on the stage, fast asleep: a limp, sodden puddle of a dog. The man kept repeating, with great energy and enthusiasm, "*Heee's* a-gonna DO it! *Heee's* a gonna DO it!" (The dog never did it.)

The efforts of Halycon Sage and his friends to contact you, the readers in the Alternate Universe, have been a bit like that. Oh, Sageworld has twitched in its sleep, maybe even gotten up and stretched with a musical canine yawn. But though a small and loyal following of readers and reviewers was ecstatic, the books were never really seen by their intended audience. They had no chance to race around the stage, singing Italian opera and juggling plates. Indications are that this is about to change.

Our multiverse contains fictional and real-world explorations into a kaleidoscope of intriguing characters, cultures, worldviews, thoughts, emotions, and the permeable borders between them. You can find us in

The Way Beyond and *The Book of Squidly Light* or at our website.[1] We will all be delighted to welcome you there. Remember, the Nanobots are serving sandwiches.

—The Editors

A LETTER

FROM OUR DESIGNER

Pleased as I would be to claim that this book was deliberately designed to look like a zine, motivated by a small bit of nerd knowledge linking the origin of the modern "zine" to the science fiction genre,[1] such was not, in fact, my original intention. Rather I sought a way to visually translate a blog to print while somehow incorporating design elements that would appeal to the book's audience. This was not an easy task.

You see, this collection springs from the *The Sage Chronicles*, a series which presents many complexities in classification and thereby in defining its audience. The books within it fall partially into what's called the slipstream genre,[2] while maintaining qualities that are more in line with general science fiction and also incorporating the intellectual feel of literary fiction.

---

1. The first zine is often attributed to the Science Correspondence Club in Chicago in the 1930s. It was called *The Comet* and it began a long-term trend of sci-fi zines.

2. As a developing genre, Slipstream is described as non-realistic fiction with a postmodern sensibility. It looks at authors', poets' and experimentalists' awareness of social and technological change and psychological breakdown during postmodernism and modernism.

They avoid superfluous prose in favor of a stream-of-consciousness style that resembles James Joyce or Faulkner, but is presented at a rapid pace that echoes the excited voice of Kerouac, seasoned with a dash of wit and humor which feels like Klosterman.

So I had first to consider all of this in determining—well, you dear reader—and then to take that information and apply it to building a book composed of myriad short works assembled from various characters and settings, containing multiple themes and styles from multiple viewpoints, told in several voices, and spanning many subjects in a way that mixes reality, fiction, and creativity into an intellectual—for lack of a better phrase here—Sage soup.

I drafted many layout options intended to embody my desire to create something that echoed classic literature and felt like a book, yet somehow reflected the chaos of papers scattered across the top of an editor's desk. An editor seated in an office at some sort of omnipresent helm of Sage's multiverse.

It seems the final product of such an intention can be best described as "Practically a zine"!*

---

*Author's Note: Just FYI, over the years of writing The Sage Chronicles, I wasn't consciously trying to do any of the above. This is just what it sounds like inside my head.

SAGE'S SAGA

CONTINUES...

OR BEGINS...

or MAYBE EXPANDS...

This space-time-multiverse stuff creates some degree of uncertainty...

PERHAPS IT EXTENDS?

Whatever it does, it does it in the universe within which
exists a series titled :

THE SAGE CHRONICLES

BY KARIMA VARGAS BUSHNELL

(Turn page to learn more) ⯈⯈⯈⯈

THE WAY BEYOND

Original Title *The Life and Times of Halycon Sage*

ISBN: 978-1-7334288-4-2

A story full of the sights, sounds and smells of Northern Nevada, mixed in with a bunch of crazy characters and a plot that expands in all directions from a seemingly simple beginning.

Halycon Sage, founder of the Post-Modernist Minimalist Neo-Symbolist Pseudo-Realist School of Literature, has voluntarily disappeared. He is hoping to save the world, but is also fleeing the Mail Pile.

Sage, a person of mystery who may be a Native American male, meets some odd characters:

Petulant critic Basel Vasselschnauzer, confused genius Alexander Preisczech, a Romani woman, assorted gang members and secret agents, and a shadowy figure of evil. Sage has a faithful equine companion, No-Name Stupid (the original "Horse with No Name"). But even with Stupid's dedicated assistance, can the great quest succeed? And will *Boo Radley Goes Hawaiian* ever be written?

This Third Edition, retitled *The Way Beyond*, includes revised material that brings the reader deeper into the story. You may get lost in this deceptively simple novel.

Praise for *The Life and Times of Halycon Sage*

"*The Life and Times of Halycon Sage* has the stirring immediacy of a guitar riff."
— *BlueInk Review*

"Is it genius? Is it nonsense? Sage may be the last person to know. This deliciously funny, madcap novel leaps with a frenetic energy reminiscent mid-1960s postmodernism."

— *Kirkus Review*

THE **BOOK** OF **SQUIDLY LIGHT**

ISBN: 978-1-7334288-5-9

Imaginary author Halycon Sage, founder of the Post-Modernist Minimalist Neo-Symbolist Pseudo-Realist School of Literature, returns!

Characters, themes and subplots, complex levels and layers interweave like the five-colored strands of the Braided Thread, the most sacred concept from the aliens' holy text, *The Book of Lighted Squid.* The Squids argue semantics while addressing a whole host of new problems, including the appearance of an Alternate Universe and an evil plot code-named Barbecue!

Sorrow and absurdity, mystical secrets and high adventure, sweet romance and a real attempt to save the Earth.

Praise for *The Book of Squidly Light*

"This eclectic, genre-bending novel follows *The Life and Times of Halycon Sage* [*The Way Beyond*] which introduced the eponymous Sage, a [SPOILER REMOVED] and celebrated author. Here, we find him dwelling in a world recently purged of modern technology and escaping into his writing, unaware of how his words impact a fluctuating multiverse. In a metafictional conceit worthy of a Charlie Kaufman film, it turns out that while Bushnell is the creator of Sage, Sage is the author of Bushnell and the reality—our reality—where she exists."

- Blue Ink Review
The American Library Association
Book List Magazine